The Dancer and the Dragon Speaker

LAURIE LUCKING

THE INTERTWINED TALES

CONTENTS

DEDICATION

For Martin – you have so many gifts and such a talent for influencing the people around you.
Always remember to use your powers for good, and I can't wait to see the impact you'll have on the world!

CHAPTER 1

"WILL SOMEONE FIX MY hair?" My sister Rosalind's whisper made the candle on her vanity flicker.

"In a minute." I tied the wide pink ribbon around my youngest sister's waist into a bow at the back. "All done, Pippa."

She craned her neck and smiled as I patted her shoulder. "Danil says he doesn't like pink, but it's still my favorite color."

With an effort, I kept my jaw unclenched. "Don't worry about what Danil thinks. You look lovely."

"But I do want him to think I'm pretty." Pippa swished her silk skirt with a flourish. "He's the only one I ever get to dance with."

"Only for now." I shared an uneasy look with Rose in the mirror as I crossed the room to where she sat on a cushioned stool. "Next year, you'll finally get to attend balls and parties here in Oneska. Then I'm sure you'll have dozens of dance partners."

"Not as many as Rose, I bet." At age twelve, Pippa hated being left behind with a governess while the rest of us attended social events. She twirled, then sank onto the edge of her bed.

Rose didn't bother to hide a self-satisfied smirk. "Even I don't *always* fill my dance card."

I stifled a huff. Universally acknowledged as the most beautiful of the five Oneskan princesses, a failure to fill her dance card only meant Rosalind was choosing to be coy. I pushed a jeweled pin into her hair to hold a braid in place.

Callista, three years older than Rose, faced Pippa with a smile. "We'd all have sore feet if we danced as much as Rose. Besides, with your long curls, blue eyes, and quick wit, you're sure to attract many suitors once you're old enough." She fastened a string of pearls around her neck and sat next to Pippa.

The large, hexagonal chamber we all shared had a bed, dresser, and vanity along every wall except where orange flames danced in the granite fireplace. Assorted chairs, settees, and cushions circled the thick rug at the center.

I glanced at my own reflection as I swept more of Rose's lustrous auburn curls atop her head. Straight, unremarkable hair, pale skin, lips pressed into a thin line, eyes creased with worry. No doubt the only reason any gentleman ever asked me to dance was due to my status as the Crown Princess.

"Ouch!" Rose rubbed her head where I'd been inserting another pin. "Careful with those."

"Sorry." Shaking my head in an attempt to focus my thoughts, I slowly slid the pin into her hair.

Tonight I needed to protect my sisters, not fret about my appearance.

"If only we didn't have to change into our nightclothes and get re-dressed every time." Rose heaved a dramatic sigh.

Calli gave a sympathetic nod. "It would be much easier if we could at least get help from our maids."

"But that would make them suspicious, right?" Pippa bounced on the edge of her bed.

"Exactly." Calli patted her knee, then glanced around. "Jolene, did you still need help with—?"

"Jo!" Pippa's scolding tone drowned out Calli's question. "You aren't even dressed yet."

Jolene, our second-youngest sister, sank further into the cushions on her bed. "Why do I have to go? There aren't even enough princes, and Pippa enjoys it more."

"Speaking of not making anyone suspicious..." I gave Pippa a quelling look. "We have to keep quiet in here. And Jo, we've been through this. Prince Leonnar has requested that all five of us be in attendance. You know we can't afford to...anger him."

Calli hurried across the room to Jo. "We're all tired, dear one. But it's not so bad. Maybe they'll have some of those honey cakes you like so much." Putting an arm around her shoulders, Calli helped her slide off the bed.

"But why do we have to work so hard to look nice? We don't even like them." Jo crossed her arms over her chest with a glower only a fourteen-year-old could achieve.

Rose snorted, and I covered a laugh of my own before turning around. "We're still representatives of Oneska, even in places or situations we'd rather avoid. And you'd best hurry, we don't want our *escorts* to get restless."

Rose shuddered, all traces of humor gone. "I can finish my hair. Thank you, Emelia."

I gave her a quick nod before joining Calli in pulling a dress over our reluctant sister's head.

I paused at the top of the steep, twisting stairway, my choking gasps having little to do with the level of exertion. *Breathe, Emelia.*

This hidden staircase, accessible only by climbing through a trapdoor on the ceiling of our bedchamber, exited to the roof of our tower. The narrow, cramped space had been designed as a secret escape by one of our ancestors to be used in case of assassins or revolt. *What would he think of us now?* I cringed as a stomp above made the stony structure tremble.

Calli touched my shoulder. "Do you need me to go first tonight? You're always so brave for our sakes, but I know how those creatures affect you."

"Thank you, but I'll be all right." I raised my hand to press flat against the hatch that would release us into the clutches of our worst enemies.

"It's so dark." Jolene's voice trembled behind us. She hated these nighttime excursions even more than I did.

With a nod and a fortifying breath, I pushed open the hatch and climbed through.

The night air above was crisp with hints of early autumn. Competing with only a sliver of moonlight, the stars twinkled in a merry dance above, too many to be numbered.

There's a vast universe out there, so much bigger than myself. Its Maker is watching us even now.

The comforting thought dissolved into mist when a giant head blew warm air across my face with a snort.

Stifling a scream, I scrambled onto the rooftop and moved aside for Calli to get through. Calli helped Pippa, then Jolene ascend onto the flat tower roof. Even Pippa's usual chatter fell silent in the presence of these menacing beasts. Just as well, since no one could know we weren't asleep in our beds. Rosalind exited last, somehow maintaining the bearing of a queen as she swiped a cobweb from her skirt.

Squaring my shoulders, I faced the monstrosities Prince Leonnar sent to threaten and escort us every time he desired our presence in his neighboring kingdom of Tsantar. Two dragons currently alighted on the turret, their massive talons scraping against the dark stone. Three more circled above, like giant birds of prey.

The dragon that seemed to consider itself assigned to me stood to my right. With scales a deep indigo, wings extending from its back that curved like a pair of giant mainsails, and pointed horns like a regal gazelle, the creature could almost be viewed as majestic. If it were flying at a distance, perhaps, or as the subject of a painting.

But with each jagged scale on full display and Prince Leonnar's warnings crowding my mind, I couldn't mistake this creature for anything but what it was. A monster coiled and ready to destroy everything I loved with its searing fire and slashing talons.

The dragon swiveled its long neck to regard me with round, silver eyes. Wondering what was taking me so long, no doubt. Yet as it blinked, something almost like pity seemed to soften its intent gaze.

I recoiled at the thought with a bitter internal laugh. These monsters had no pity for us, nor anyone in this kingdom they plagued. With a sniff, I scrambled up the dragon's rigid spines to perch on its back, ducking behind its wings. It was likely too dark for anyone to see my silhouette, but it wasn't worth the risk.

Pippa had already climbed onto her red-scaled dragon, making space for Calli's dragon with golden-yellow scales.

My dragon gave its wings a flap, and I clung tighter as we lifted from the turret. My stomach always seemed to remain behind on the palace roof, leaving me dizzy and nauseous. I squinted into the wind kicked up by so many pairs of beating wings to see Jolene, then Rosalind mount their own dragons.

Then we were off. Out over the palace city of Gryfadele, past the cliffs of Lake Lohanna, above a dense forest, to the rocky coast of Tsantar.

Tears stung my eyes as I buried my face against unrelenting scales. Would we never be free?

"QkAuNz."

The harsh, guttural call sent shivers down my spine as effectively as the cool, salt-tinged autumn wind whipping through my thin shawl. Before I could pause to think, my head raised from my dragon's neck to glance down at Yrtulk Citadel. In the darkness, its tall, pointed spires resembled sharp, fierce mountain peaks. Light glowed from each porthole-shaped window like a forge lit from within, reflecting in glittering shards on the lapping ocean beyond.

It seemed no one in the citadel bothered to sleep when Prince Leonnar threw one of his many parties.

The Crown Prince himself stood on a large, semi-circular balcony, his face lit in an eerie glow by the torch his servant held aloft. He presented a regal picture, his broad chest and shoulders encased in embroidered brocade of a deep blue and his thick, dark blond hair tied back with a leather strap. His sharp jawline and full lips would be almost handsome, if not for the prideful, careless glint that always shone in his gray eyes.

He raised an arm. *"OeFlAnJp."*

I winced, my stomach lurching as my dragon changed its trajectory to descend toward Prince Leonnar's balcony. Turning my head in a jerky movement, I verified that each of my sisters' mounts had done the same. My eyelids squeezed closed just as Indigo Scales alighted on the dark, silver-threaded charcoal stone unique to Tsantar. We came to a stop with a thump, its wings flexing a few times before folding at its sides.

Suppressing a groan, I slid to the ground. I'd managed to keep my dinner lodged as a lump in my stomach, but I had no interest in sampling any of the delicacies that would be served at tonight's festivities. The balcony trembled as each of my sisters' dragons landed with a clatter of talons.

Shrouded in my dragon's shadow, I inhaled one deep breath. Two. *Time to dance, Emelia.* I nearly let a bitter laugh escape. To think I used to enjoy lilting around a ballroom floor in time with the music. But far beyond the physical activity, of which Prince Leonnar would require plenty, it was the mental dance that would leave me exhausted when he finally released us to endure another nauseating flight home in the hours just before dawn.

The wordplay, the tightrope walk of defying Leonnar in whatever small ways I could without angering him enough to command his dragons to raze our beloved Kavalya Palace to the ground. Or the entire country of Oneska, like they'd done to Philistra...

A course of action he'd threatened often enough.

With one last shuddering breath, I straightened my coral satin skirt and stepped away from my dragon. Jolene hovered nearby, cowering as Peach Scales huffed and snapped at an evening jay soaring above. I hurried to her, nearly tripping on her mount's light orange tail.

"We made it." The assurance was as much for myself as for my sister.

She wrapped her arms around one of mine. "I hate this place."

I patted her hand. "Me too. But we'll be strong for Oneska and for Father. It's just another night of dancing. There could be worse forms of captivity."

"Maybe." Her light-brown brows furrowed above her dark eyes. "Prison might be preferable, if they let me keep my harp and crochet hooks."

"I'd request books instead, but I know what you mean." I snuggled against her for a moment before straightening. "Come on, before someone hears us and decides to let us give the dungeons a try."

"If we must." Heaving a sigh, she walked at my side to where Pippa chatted with Prince Leonnar, Calli regarded her with fond amusement, and Rosalind fixed her windswept hair.

"Princess Emelia, there you are. I was hoping you'd join us this evening." Leonnar swept out a hand in welcome, as though he'd sent us an embossed invitation via royal messenger rather than a set of fire-breathing dragons.

I disentangled my arm from Jolene and stepped forward. "You know I couldn't miss one of your gatherings, Prince Leonnar."

"Indeed." A warning shone behind the glimmer of sardonic humor in his eyes. "Please, do come in. I hate to neglect my guests, and my brothers await the company of your fair sisters. We wouldn't want you to get a chill in this cool night air."

"A sneezing princess makes a poor excuse for a dancing partner." Holding my shoulders erect, I stepped forward and took his offered arm.

"My thoughts exactly." He glanced behind us as my sisters filed inside, Calli leading Jolene and Pippa chatting with Rose.

While I'd rather be anywhere else, the absence of the nipping wind did make my shivering subside. I pulled my shawl tighter with my free hand. "Your parties seem to become more frequent all the time. What is tonight's occasion?"

"Ah, I must've neglected to tell you. Tonight we celebrate Matvey's seventeenth birthday. He can hardly enjoy the occasion fully until lovely Rosalind is at his side." He kept his grip on my arm as we descended a winding staircase with gleaming silver handrails.

I swallowed a snort. Leonnar never told us when we would be summoned next, no doubt to keep us in anxious suspense. "Prince Matvey is one of many admirers Rosalind has gathered in recent years."

"I hope she considers my brother as a top candidate for her hand." He leveled a pointed look in my direction. "After all, you've seen how much Tsantar has to offer as an ally. Access to our ports, exotic delicacies from the sea. A flight of dragons as allies, rather than foes..." He cleared his throat. "It's no small consideration."

Yes, that point had been driven home effectively. Every time he threatened destruction by dragon fire if we were to tell anyone about our forced trips to Tsantar. Each mention of Philistra, the island that had been decimated by Tsantarian dragons over a decade before when they dared stand up to their larger neighbor.

"In return for our timber and crops and iron reserves. As you've pointed out, the partnership wouldn't be without benefits." Benefits that couldn't begin to outweigh the drawbacks. "But Rosalind is only sixteen. Hardly old enough to give marriage any serious thought. She has plenty of time to make her choice."

"While you, perhaps, do not."

His words lodged into my heart like a burr. At twenty-one, the marriage queries and suggestions had become less and less subtle. But I'd yet to meet anyone I'd have any interest in spending my life with. And even if I had, how would Leonnar retaliate if I chose another with such finality?

Not that the man even liked me, but he seemed determined to keep me—all of us—at his beck and call. To parade us around, as though Oneska and Tsantar had forged the closest of ties.

Before I could formulate a response, music and laughter spilled from a bright room ahead. As we continued down the torch-lit hall, I tried to ignore the murals of dragons raining fire down upon thatch-roofed homes or bearing armor-clad soldiers into war.

Clearly, we weren't the first kingdom Tsantar had tyrannized with its dragon throng.

Our steps slowed, the rustling of my sisters' dancing slippers shuffling to a halt behind us. Prince Leonnar puffed out his chest, directing one last glare my way before pasting on a smile and stepping through the doorframe. "My friends, look who came to join us this evening!"

A few indistinct calls of welcome greeted our entrance. Though I'd spent more hours in this ballroom than I cared to count, the first view always made me blink. Vibrant scarves of every color bedecked the walls, and chandeliers brimming with candles hung every few feet, lighting the space with an almost garish glow.

The younger three Tsantarian princes strode forward, saluting my sisters with stiff bows.

I attempted a smile of my own as I stepped further inside and scanned the room filled with elegantly clad nobility, all dancing, mingling, or heaping sweets onto silver-edged plates.

Time for the dance to begin.

CHAPTER 2

"I can tell something weighs on your mind." Prince Leonnar turned me in a circle before resuming his grasp on my waist.

I didn't bother to turn my snort into a delicate cough like I would've at one of our own events in Oneska. "Something usually does. But not often anything you'd like to hear, I imagine."

He shook his head. "Always so begrudging of my hospitality." We shifted our rhythmic steps to the side to allow a twirling couple to pass.

I arched to my toes every few steps, trying to ignore my aching feet. *Thank goodness we don't host balls in Oneska nearly as often as we're required to attend them here.* "Hospitality and captivity must hold very similar meanings in Tsantar."

He spun me away in synchronization with the other dancers before pulling me closer. "It all depends on your perspective, dear Emelia."

My jaw tightened until a headache sprang to my temples. "My perspective is that I'd much rather be at home, resting."

"How very dull that sounds." Leonnar's smile would've almost been charming if I'd never met him before. "And you'd miss the opportunity to consort with our new guests, the Tsar and Tsarina of Khadijah."

"Did they get monstrous *escorts*, too?" I inserted as much venom into the whisper as I could.

His laugh expressed delight rather than fear or remorse. "I reserve that privilege only for you and your lovely sisters." He tweaked my chin in a revoltingly intimate gesture. "I'll introduce you to them later, if you promise to behave yourself. I'd hate to have to instruct my dragons to do more than escort you, after all."

If only I could scream and rail at the helpless corner he'd backed us into with those cursed dragons. *Breathe, Emelia. Keep up with the steps, don't remove your mask.* I glanced to the couple he'd indicated, who danced with fluid motions in their brightly-colored tunics. "I'd be happy to make their acquaintance, but preferably not under the pretense of being your ally."

"Must it remain a pretense? Am I truly so repulsive that you can't even consider the possibility of becoming my queen?" His tone almost sounded convincingly hurt.

Almost.

"How long do you plan to toy with me before you force my hand?" My feet faltered. The question had plagued me for months, but what had possessed me to voice it aloud? What if he pounced at the opportunity? *You can't let your guard down, Emelia.* If only I could shake my exhausted mind into a full state of alertness to avoid such blunders.

"I'd hate for it to come to that, but I can understand why you ask." He eased us back into rhythm with the practiced steps of a prince who did little other than attend balls and parties. "How much do you know about Tsantarian wedding ceremonies?"

"There's magic invsolved." Speaking the frightening idea aloud made my mouth dry. "It produces some kind of...mind-sharing." *No.*

It must never come to that. Such a coerced invasion of my very consciousness was bound to drive me mad.

"Indeed." He nodded as though I were a clever pupil. "But the mind-sharing, as you call it, can only be completed in a union that is...willing. If I were to force you, we would never get to experience the full closeness the union intends."

I bit back a cry of triumph. *That's* why he was stuck with his twisted attempts to court me without threatening a wedding. He could never gain the secrets of our kingdom if I didn't want to marry him. Tempting as it was to gloat, I settled for, "I see."

"It's not as impossible as you think." He must've detected some of my relief, despite my attempts to keep my expression passive. "Even if you never fall prey to my own charms, you have four sisters after all."

My scoff dissolved as I followed his gaze to where Rosalind whispered in Matvey's ear, looking into his eyes with batting lashes. Small wonder he wanted Rosalind's glowing beauty and bold coquetry as part of his birthday celebration. But while Rosalind enjoyed flirting, she was too smart to actually fall for one of the Tsantarian princes.

Wasn't she?

I glimpsed Calli giving her escort a gentle smile. But she was gracious to everyone, and she'd been spending increasing amounts of time with Duke Virkalt. Her heart, at least, should be safe.

Jolene stood at the edge of the dance floor, back as ramrod straight as any soldier. I nearly giggled at the sight. The poor girl detested everything about our excursions to Tsantar, from the dragon rides to the forced proximity of a crowded ballroom. She'd expressed on countless occasions her gratitude that Prince Leonnar only had three brothers so she could sit out most of the dances. They'd never find a willing marriage there.

But Pippa... The suppressed giggle burst like a popped soap bubble. She laughed with Danil, standing close to his side as they clapped for the assortment of string, wind, and percussion instruments ending the tune. She'd enthused about Danil on several occasions over the past few weeks. He was apparently funny, smart, and an excellent dancer. Though in her sheltered life, not yet allowed to attend our own banquets, she had little to compare him with.

I winced. He did seem to treat her kindly, but what secrets would he be pressured to share with Prince Leonnar and his father if they were to become a true match someday?

"Something to think about, isn't it?" Leonnar already faced me for another dance but seemed pleased, rather than irritated, by my distraction.

No. We would rid ourselves of the dragons somehow. None of my sisters would fall prey to mind-control by the Tsantarian royal family if I had anything to do with it.

"Not those infernal creatures again." Father's once jolly voice was sounding more like a growl all the time.

"Come sit down, Father." Exhaustion dampened my wheedling tone. The poor man obsessively checked the skies at every hour of the day. We'd specifically chosen this spot to sit with him in the gardens after dinner because tall, closely-crowded trees blocked the view of the palace.

But at the moment, he was pushing aside the gardeners' handiwork with his walking stick to peer into the fading evening light.

"Have you ever seen a flower this vibrant? Father, you must be sure to compliment Jeno." Calli touched a bright orange blossom with a smile. Jeno had haunted these gardens for as long as we could remember, as gray and wiry as he was spry.

Father ignored her, pushing farther into the trees. Beside me, Jolene's crochet hooks stilled as she frowned toward him.

I nudged her. "Keep going. I want to see how that reticule turns out once you've added all the colors."

Smile still in place, Calli released the flower. She crossed to Father and rested a hand on his shoulder. "We know it's been a trying time, Father. But you'll make yourself ill if you don't relax and get some rest."

"Relaxation will not rid our kingdom of these cursed dragons." Tension punctuated his every word. "Look there, if you don't believe me!"

Calli's gaze snapped to the thin part in the trees, and her shoulders tightened.

Not again. The ball with the Khadijan royals had taken place only two days before.

I caught Rosalind's eye from her adjoining bench. Resignation pinched her lovely features. Jolene set down her project and stared down at Pippa, likely willing her not to say anything.

"It's not that we don't believe you, Father." I joined Calli in tugging him away from the gap he'd created in the trees. His arm felt less substantial through the stiff velvet of his jacket than it had only weeks before. "We understand how much the dragons' presence plagues you." More than he could possibly know. "But allowing your own health to fail won't make them go away."

"No." His entire body trembled as he wrenched himself from our grasp. "But it's time to do something that will. Rhoden." He gestured to the guard hovering farther down the garden path. "Where is Atticus?"

Rhoden's brows rose. "Likely in his chamber, Your Majesty."

"Atticus? After the dinner hour, Father?" Callista's gentle tone held no rebuke, only surprise.

I frowned. Usually, Father only summoned his Royal Clerk when he was working in his office on business like treaty negotiations or agricultural reports. Why would he need him now, with such urgency?

Father stomped down the path, sending little clouds of dirt puffing into the air in his wake. "I've a proclamation to make that can't wait a moment longer."

"A proclamation?" I hurried to follow, nearly tripping on my billowing skirts. "But wouldn't it be wise to call your Council together in the morning? Surely it can't be so urgent as to—"

"There's no need, my mind is made up." He quickened his pace, not bothering to see whether we could keep up.

I exchanged concerned glances with my sisters. Prince Leonnar had first sent the dragons to plague our kingdom two seasons ago, accompanied by instructions from a Tsantarian spy who'd infiltrated our palace as a lady's maid. Every time Leonnar wanted us to attend one of his events, which seemed to become more frequent all the time, his monsters weaved around the turrets at dusk, circling the castle until we could ride away on their backs under cover of darkness.

Their mysterious presence had nearly driven our poor father to distraction. The Tsantarian prince had forbidden us from telling anyone of our nighttime excursions, sparing no detail of what the dragons would do to our palace should we fail to comply.

Even if we did tell Father, surely it would only change the nature of his angst. Instead of wondering why the dragons insisted on returning to Kavalya Palace, he might instead try something foolish like declaring war on Tsantar.

I rubbed my forehead, bracing myself for a long night ahead. What could've changed so suddenly that Father now thought he had a plan for the dragons' removal? And what kind of danger might it create for Oneska?

"Atticus. There you are." Father's voice held an eerie note of relief after his rigid march into the palace and through the corridors to the servants' quarters.

We'd trailed him in grim silence, Jolene's face pinched as though fighting tears after we'd walked far enough to confirm that the dragons truly had returned. Already.

"I have a proclamation to make." Father held his head high, his dark hair interspersed with gray a bit windswept from our time outdoors.

"A proclamation? Right now?" Atticus's broad shoulders filled his doorframe. He blinked and shook his head, his cream-colored jacket clean but a bit rumpled. Perhaps he was already making bedtime preparations or had been absorbed in a riveting book.

A few curious servants had gathered in the hall. I gave them a tight smile and nod. Whispering among themselves, they shuffled farther back to the stairwell.

I couldn't guess what Father had in mind, but the fewer witnesses, the better.

"Indeed. It involves those cursed dragons, after all. When better than while they're circling our very palace?" Father accentuated his point by clanging the tip of his walking stick onto the polished wooden flooring.

A few neighboring doors opened, faces pinched with concern or annoyance peeking out.

Atticus cleared his throat. "Why don't you come inside?" He began to gesture at his chamber, until his gaze landed on the rest of us hovering behind Father.

Calli dropped her arm that had been around Jolene's shoulders and stepped forward. "Perhaps if we met in your study, Father, we might be more comfortable."

"Excellent idea." Atticus hurried out of his room, closing the door behind him.

Pippa sidled up to me as we returned to the crystalline wall sconces and gilt-edged paintings of the royal wing of the palace. "This won't make us late, will it? Wouldn't that anger the dragons?"

"I hope not." I tried to keep the grumble out of my whisper. None of this was Pippa's fault, after all. "At least, not as much as whatever Father plans to say in this proclamation."

Her eyes widened. "Is he going to tell people to shoot at them?"

I'd wondered the same thing. But surely even in his tense state, Father couldn't be so foolish. "Father certainly wants to be rid of them, but I don't think anything we could shoot would pierce those scales." I scrunched my nose into what I hoped was a teasing, lighthearted expression. "That really would make them angry, wouldn't it?"

She nodded. "And I think Danil would be disappointed not to dance with me anymore."

My heart squeezed. So far Pippa harbored merely a girlish fancy for Danil, but if our forced visits to Tsantar were to continue for months, or even years... "I'm sure he would. But just remember, if you were to disappear off to Tsantar, many people here would miss you terribly."

"True." She glanced at me, and her bouncing steps faltered. "I can tell you're worried, you know. I'll get ready extra fast tonight."

"Thanks, Pippa." I brushed a strand of her light hair back into place as we filed into Father's study.

"Now, then." Father strode to the open space in front of the fireplace. My sisters and I quietly took seats on the hard wooden chairs, and Atticus hastily dug out a quill and parchment.

"I've consulted with the palace guards about these vile creatures more times than I can count. All they ever have to say for themselves is that it's too dangerous to launch an attack, or perhaps they'll leave on their own. Well, clearly they're not leaving on their own, and I want a real solution." Father's voice softened. "It hasn't escaped my notice that even my daughters haven't been sleeping well since they made their first appearance." He placed a hand on Rosalind's head, who sat nearest to him.

My gaze met Calli's, her eyes mirroring my concern. We'd had little opportunity to sleep at all on some of the nights we were summoned to Tsantar. But we'd tried so hard to hide our fatigue or make other excuses.

Father had been distracted and irritable about the dragons, but he'd always been kind and attentive toward us. All the more so after our mother had died seven years before from a fever.

I should've known he wouldn't be fooled.

"So it's time to give these men some real incentive. To let all of Oneska know that I don't take their safety or peace of mind lightly." He gave Atticus a pointed look, and the clerk poised his quill on the parchment. "Let the proclamation read... His Majesty, King Halcyon of Oneska, places the safety of his people and the royal city of Gryfadele in highest regard. No threat of any kind will be allowed to undermine the peace and security of the Oneskan people, whether from man or beast. A set of five dragons..."

My posture relaxed as he went on to describe the sightings of the dragons, pausing every few words to let Atticus keep up. Perhaps this proclamation would be nothing more than an official statement detailing his dislike of the dragons and desire to be free of them. But just as my shoulders made contact with the curved back of my chair, his words seized my full attention.

"...reward for his efforts ridding our kingdom of this plague. Therefore, I hereby declare that any man who can cause, by whatever means necessary, these dragons to never again return to Kavalya Palace, may marry whichever of my daughters he chooses and thereby become a royal prince of Oneska."

Atticus dropped his quill at the same moment Jolene fell out of her chair.

CHAPTER 3

"Wʜᴀᴛ ɪꜰ ʜᴇ's ᴀs old as Father?"

"What if he has marks all over his face like Lord Piers?"

"Ugh, what if he *is* Lord Piers?"

"Do you think Duke Virkalt will try for your hand, Calli?"

"I wouldn't mind if Prince Gregor from Therraci took on the dragons."

I struggled to pull a tiny loop of thread around one of the pearl buttons adorning the back of Calli's burgundy dress. My hands, perhaps my entire body, had been trembling ever since we left Father's study to return to our chamber. My sisters' speculations about the potential identity and characteristics of our imagined rescuer buzzed around the room like a swarm of flies, only increasing my nauseating dizziness. I finished with Calli's buttons in numb silence, then moved to my own preparations.

Questions bubbled through my own mind as quickly as they spilled from my sisters' mouths. The possibility of any of us being forced to marry whatever man succeeded in Father's challenge, no matter his identity, made my chest squeeze tighter than any stays. But I couldn't afford to dwell on that yet.

With such a *reward* dangled in front of them, what desperate measures would these men attempt in order to rid our kingdom of the dragons? And what would the dragons do in retaliation?

I shuddered, dropping the necklace I'd been fumbling to clasp about my neck. Crouching, I grazed my fingertips across the thick rug until I felt a metallic chain. Much as I wanted the foul creatures far from Kavalya Palace, I couldn't envision any method of driving them away that would succeed. No one had, or the dragons would've been disposed of or sent off months ago.

Instead, unsuccessful attempts were likely to pile up far faster and higher than before. How much would the dragons tolerate before they lost patience and—?

My throat constricted in a silent laugh-turned-sob. No one could claim the prize if the Oneskan princesses had all been burned to ash.

I clung to Indigo Scales, my eyes shut tight. If only I could wake up and find this entire evening had been nothing more than a nightmare.

The dragons began their descent, and I swallowed back bile. I'd debated with myself throughout the flight but come to no resolution. I could tell Prince Leonnar about Father's proclamation. Warn him to call off his dragons before they were injured or killed. But what if he or one of his brothers came to Oneska to claim one of our hands in marriage? What if he chose Pippa, as the most likely to willingly consent?

Tears pricked my eyes as we alighted on the balcony of Yrtulk Citadel, the sea beyond glinting in the moonlight like the sheen of a polished dagger. Cold and harsh in its beauty.

Maker, free us.

"*SmOeCx.*" Leonnar's use of the ugly, grating language the dragons understood usually made me want to cover my ears.

This time, I perked up as I slid from Indigo Scales's back.

"*IyFlOeWd, GtAuSmOe.*" Calli's golden dragon rose back into the sky, followed by Pippa's vibrant red mount.

GtAuSmOe. I tried to impress the strange combination of syllables into my mind, roll them on my tongue. *GtAuSmOe.* What if I could—?

Prince Leonnar approached, sending the thought skittering to a halt. "Good evening, Princess Emelia."

"Good evening." The fake pleasantry tasted sour in my mouth. "It seems you've had much to celebrate in recent weeks. Didn't we just attend a party a few nights back?"

He directed me through the wide, glass-paned double doors. "Indeed you did, I'm glad to hear it made an impression."

I blinked into the sudden brightness of the torches lining the walls, suppressing a bitter laugh. As though being forced to leave home late at night to attend an event in a foreign kingdom could fail to be memorable.

He paused to watch my sisters enter behind us. "But yes, the Khadijan Tsar and Tsarina will grace us with their presence a few days longer. We must make their stay as enjoyable as possible."

"Ah, of course." Based on our conversation at the last party, the Khadijan leaders were full of their own self-importance and swatted at servants like pesky bugs. No wonder they got along so well with Prince Leonnar.

"I hope you do not mind the frequency of our invitations. Our events would not be the same without the lovely Oneskan princesses."

I lifted my skirt to descend the curving grand stairway, hoping my grinding teeth couldn't be heard above the clacking of Leonnar's boots and the din of the party below. *Don't let him goad you, Emelia. Focus on what's important.* Heaving a deep breath, I sent up a quick prayer for wisdom. Best to get this out of the way before we were surrounded by the distractions of the ballroom.

"While I do appreciate that sentiment, do you think it wise to *invite* us so often?" My free hand gripped the silver banister.

"Whatever do you mean?" He peered at my face with genuine curiosity.

"As you know, not everyone in Oneska understands the friendly nature of the invitations your dragons seek to impart." I tried to keep the irony out of my tone, dancing the thin line between getting the answers I needed without revealing too much information. "As a result, the increasing frequency of their visits has caused some people around Kavalya Palace, my father included, to view them as a threat."

"Is that so?" The irritating man responded as though I were commenting on the weather.

My worn-out slipper nearly skated off the final stair. "I fear this misunderstanding might cause harm to your dragons, if someone tried to eliminate them in an ill-advised attempt to protect our kingdom."

Prince Leonnar's laughter echoed through the expansive hall. "How kind of you to fear for my dragons, dear Emelia." He patted my hand in a patronizing gesture that made my spine stiffen. "But nothing your knights could launch at my cherished pets could cause them any damage. Whether it might anger them, on the other hand..." He raised his arms in an exaggerated shrug.

I pressed my lips together, his words bringing my worst fears to the surface. "Perhaps if you lessened the frequency of our visits? Surely a few occasions per month would be enough to flaunt our presence to your court and whatever guests you—"

"Ah, but what of the growing affection between Danil and sweet Pippa? Or Matvey and lovely Rosalind? Even Radimir seems to be growing fond of dear Callista. I'd hate to deprive my brothers of their company. And where would I be, without such a skilled dancing partner at my side?"

I refused to flinch at the challenge in his eyes. "No doubt I would be even more skilled as a partner if I had more opportunities to rest. And wouldn't it be better for the relationship between our kingdoms if there wasn't any ugliness resulting from your *pets* losing their tempers? Perhaps an opportunity to miss each other would only increase the fondness between your brothers and my sisters." My stomach clenched at the very thought.

His smile still glinted with dark humor. "You are too young yet to prefer rest when there are balls and banquets to attend, Princess Emelia." Leaning closer, he lowered his voice. "And you are clever and resourceful, are you not? Surely you can find a way to dissuade your father and the others from taking actions that might cause more harm to your beloved Kavalya Palace than to my dragons. The safety of your very kingdom may depend upon it."

I willed the fear to stay out of my eyes as everything within me recoiled. But as Leonnar tugged me into the ballroom, his entire demeanor changing to gregarious hospitality, a resolve settled within my core. I *would* find a way to protect my kingdom. But not by convincing my father and his knights to leave the dragons alone.

By getting rid of them myself.

Where is she? My horse, Lyuda, snuffled my hair. With a giggle, I swatted her away. "I know. I'm impatient to be on our way as well."

She snorted and tossed her head. I gripped her bridle, running my fingers down the white streak on her forehead that stood out against her otherwise dark brown coat.

Calli had agreed to meet me for a ride this morning. I wanted to discuss something with her that I didn't want overheard. But she was running unusually late.

"Here, you silly thing." Lyuda was nuzzling my shoulder this time, so I tugged her reins and brought her to a new patch of grass.

Calli's sweet, clear laughter rang out across the field. I shaded my eyes to squint in the direction of the palace, and two forms came into view. Calli, smiling and radiant in a dark green riding dress, her golden-brown hair spilling over her shoulder, and a gentleman wearing a crisp gray jacket and matching breeches that disappeared into black riding boots.

Ah, no wonder she's delayed. Duke Virkalt had been frequenting Kavalya Palace more and more often lately, and he always found an excuse to approach my gentle sister.

From what I could tell, Calli didn't mind a bit.

"That would be delightful. I do so love music." Calli smiled up at the tall Duke, her arm wrapped more tightly around his than was strictly necessary when being escorted by a gentleman.

"Then I shall look forward to it." He clasped her hand. "Speaking of music, will I get to hear you sing again sometime soon? Your rendition of Starlit Garden was the best I've ever heard it performed."

Calli's cheeks pinked. "You are too kind. But our cousin, the Earl of Renitsa, is coming to visit soon. Father will likely invite us to sing, with Jolene accompanying on her harp. I'm sure he would be thrilled for you to join us."

At least Callista's heart seemed plenty safe from any of the Tsantarian princes. I pulled Lyuda's reins, but she kept her head down, determinedly munching on grass. "Come on, Lyuda." Her ears barely flicked at my low whisper. "Let's go back to the stable before—"

"Em! I'm so sorry, I must be late."

I straightened, suppressing a grimace. Apparently, we'd already been spotted. "No trouble at all, it's a beautiful morning. Good to see you again, Your Grace."

Duke Virkalt smiled and bowed. "Princess Emelia. I hope you're well."

"I am, thank you. And your family?"

"It's kind of you to ask, they're very well. My sister joined me on this visit. I'm sure she'd appreciate an opportunity to get to know all of you better." His eyes lingered on Calli.

Calli's smile grew broader, if such a thing were possible. "I'm eager to see her again." She tore her gaze away from her suitor to focus on me. "Emelia and I were planning on a ride this morning. Would you like to join us?"

I fought to keep my expression neutral as he glanced to me. We'd never have a chance to discuss the dragon problem if Calli's Duke was going to follow her everywhere.

"No, thank you. I came to check on my own horse and put him through some paces, and I have no wish to intrude on your time together." He nodded to me. "But perhaps you would join me for luncheon? My sister and I thought a picnic in the gardens might be nice."

"Thank you, I'd like that very much." Calli squeezed his arm, then let go. "I'll find you later."

"I shall look forward to it." He bowed and headed to the stables, glancing back at Calli several times in the process.

"Tania is already saddled. They tied her up over here." I led Calli to a shaded area of the paddock, where her sleek white horse awaited us. Lyuda trotted ahead, apparently now more than happy to move. I leaned toward Calli. "Sorry for the interruption. Lyuda refused to be dragged away from that patch of grass."

"She can be an obstinate one." If any of our younger sisters were present, no doubt they would've made a comparison to Lyuda's rider. "But it was no interruption at all! I hope you and Theon will have more opportunities to get to know each other."

My chest constricted. I was thrilled Calli had found someone who appreciated her and treated her well, but I wasn't ready to lose my closest sister anytime soon. "I suppose I'd better spend some time with him to make sure he deserves you. It's hard to imagine anyone could."

"Oh, stop." She swatted at my arm, then ducked her red cheeks behind Tania. "We enjoy spending time together, but nothing beyond that at present."

"Picnics, a concert..." I feigned a wince. "I wonder whether Rose or Pippa will squeal louder."

She laughed as she swung into the saddle. "Hopefully neither."

I mounted Lyuda, and we took off toward our favorite dirt trail through the forest. We rode in silence for a time, only the rhythmic clopping of our horses' hooves interrupting the keening crickets and chattering birds.

We reached a clearing at the top of a hill, and Calli rotated Tania to take in the view. I pulled Lyuda to a stop beside her.

Calli turned to me, her self-conscious flush replaced by worry lines. "You said you wanted to speak with me about something? I'm assuming it involves Father's proclamation?"

"In a way, yes." I glanced in every direction, but it seemed we had this portion of the forest to ourselves. "Let's sit."

We dismounted and tied our horses where they could graze, then I chose a stump and Calli sat across from me on a fallen log. She raised her brows expectantly.

I leaned my elbows on my knees and kept my voice low. "Much as I hate the thought of just any man claiming one of our hands in marriage, I'm more concerned about how the dragons might react. What if knights start throwing spears or shooting arrows at them? I doubt it would even perforate their scales, but in response..."

"They could become violent." Calli nibbled on her lower lip. "I hadn't thought of that, but you're right. Should we tell Father the truth? I know Prince Leonnar would be furious if he found out, but perhaps it's worth the risk."

"I'm hoping it won't come to that." I scooted forward, a flicker of excitement speeding my pulse. "I had an idea. What if *we* could communicate with the dragons? Enough to make them understand that we don't wish to be taken to Tsantar, or even to command them ourselves?"

Calli's eyes widened. "They do seem to follow Prince Leonnar's instructions without hesitation. I'd never considered whether that could work for someone else. But we don't know the first thing about the dragon language, if that's even what it is."

"But we hear Prince Leonnar speak it all the time." I stood, unable to sit still any longer. "Last night, I started paying attention to the words he uses. If we all learn them, we might be able to take charge when they're on our tower roof. Possibly even send them away."

"Oh, I do hope you're right. To be able to end this mess without any destruction or bloodshed..." She rose and gripped my arms. "Let's start right now."

CHAPTER 4

"Eflop." Calli's shoulders drooped.

We'd spent the past half hour in the clearing, but she'd made no progress on either of the two words I'd attempted to teach her. Somehow, her melodic voice couldn't capture the guttural resonance of the dragon language.

"That's closer." I tried to keep my tone upbeat. Maybe she'd finally get it on the fiftieth try? I wanted to sink my face into my hands and give up. If Calli, usually the quickest to pick up on things among my sisters, couldn't even pronounce this one word properly, my plan seemed doomed to failure already.

I might be able to command all the dragons myself, but it would give us far less flexibility. And be far more dangerous. What if a dragon flew off with one of my sisters while I struggled to communicate with the others?

Choking back my doubts, I pasted on a smile. It was too soon to give up yet. "Let's try again. Remember the letters seem to come in pairs. Draw out the first syllable, then the other two are choppier. *OeFlAnJp.*"

"Oiflap?" It rose at the end like a question. Calli's pout was half comic, half tragic.

"Let's try a different one." I gazed at the halo of fiery red leaves just above us, letting nature's beauty soothe my frustration. Blowing out a breath, I gave my sister an encouraging smile. "Can you say *SmOeCx?* I think it means something like stop."

"Smocks." Close, but with none of the vowel blending that made their words sound so foreign. Calli sank back onto her log. "I'm sorry, Em. I really am trying, but I just don't think—"

"Excuse me."

I started at the appearance of a man riding a palomino mare. His bronzed face seemed tense, as though it took some effort to keep his pleasant expression wrangled into place. A shock of light brown hair fringed his forehead beneath a gray cap.

Had he overheard us? How had I let myself get so distracted that I missed his approach?

I straightened, assuming my most formal posture. "Yes?"

He opened his mouth but gave no response, as though he'd been hoping for more to work with. The horse shifted beneath him as he swallowed. "I apologize if I startled you. I was just riding through, but you seemed quite absorbed in your conversation. Eavesdropping was the furthest from my intentions, but were you... Was that *CxIyVhAuNz* you were speaking?"

I tilted my head, trying to identify the word. "*CxIyVhAuNz?*"

"The"—he ducked his head, his voice growing softer—"the language of the dragons."

Questions bombarded my mind in a whirlwind of panic and curiosity. How did he recognize it? What might he suspect? Did he—?

"Are you familiar with it too, then? Perhaps you can help us." Calli rose to her feet, all bright smiles and innocence. "Or rather, me. Emelia is so very clever."

I gritted my teeth, forcing my expression to stay neutral. How could I signal her to be cautious without catching the stranger's attention?

"Oh, but where are my manners? I'm Princess Callista, and this is Crown Princess Emelia of Oneska." She always added a regal tone when pronouncing my title, as though it somehow dwarfed her own position just because I happened to be two years older.

The man's eyes had grown comically wide during Calli's pronouncement. He dismounted in haste, nearly catching his boot on the stirrup. "I hadn't realized...that is, forgive me—" He lowered into an awkward bow, reins clenched in his fist.

"There is nothing to forgive." Calli waved her hand like a benevolent fairy. "Are you new to Oneska, or at least to the palace?"

"I am. That is, I've been working in the stables for several weeks, Your Highness." He straightened the dark green vest he'd laced over his loose, white long-sleeved shirt, seeming to regain some measure of composure.

"Welcome. It appears you're doing an admirable job already. Your riding posture is excellent." Calli beamed at him as though he were the first man cunning enough to successfully ride a horse. "And please, call me Callista."

At this rate, the poor man would be half in love with Calli before the conversation was out. He was handsome, despite his simple, dusty attire, and admittedly his riding stance had suggested ample experience for someone who couldn't be more than five years my senior. But why did she feel the need to be so friendly toward a stable hand?

"I am Merric." He coughed and snatched his hat with his free hand. "At your service."

I bit my cheek to contain a grin. Clearly the man had little experience with royalty.

"Merric. What an interesting name. You are not from Oneska?" If Calli continued to smile at this handsome stranger, her Duke might have reason to feel jealous.

He shuffled, his horse bending to sniff his disheveled hair. "Not originally, no. But it has been my home for some time now."

"Where did you spend your childhood?" Calli took a step forward, her curls shining in the sunlight filtering through the trees. "I'm always eager to learn more about neighboring countries, in case it gives us ideas for how we can better the lives of our own people."

"Very noble of you, but I wouldn't presume to... That is, I've lived in a number of places." His smile was as tight as his grip on the reins, as though he were ready to hop back on the horse and bolt away.

But before he did, I had to get past Calli's pleasantries to the real question. "How do you know about...*CxIyVhAuNz*, you called it? The dragon language?"

He turned to me, and I nearly stumbled back as our gazes collided. His face was handsome, but his eyes were almost mesmerizing. A shade of gold-tinged-green I'd never encountered. "I—I came across it in the midst of my travels. Certainly an unusual language."

"Indeed." I studied him, searching for signs that he wasn't telling the full truth.

He quirked a brow, his tone cautious. "Are there dragons in Oneska? I thought they generally lived farther south."

I pressed my clenched fist into the folds of my riding skirt. "There shouldn't be."

He flinched. My voice must've come out as more of a growl than I intended.

"Oh, Em, we've lost track of the time! I promised to meet Theon and his sister for lunch." Calli took my arm, then faced the stable hand. "I apologize for our abrupt departure, but it was such a pleasure to meet you, Merric. I do hope our paths will cross again soon."

Merric blinked, as though he'd forgotten about Calli's presence. "Yes. That is, a pleasure to meet you both. Enjoy your ride." He bowed, following us with those green-gold eyes as we untied and mounted our horses.

The man both intrigued and annoyed me. The vague answers, his unnerving stare. Could he truly be unaware of the way dragons plagued Kavalya Palace, or was he feigning ignorance? Merric seemed to be hiding something, for what purpose I couldn't guess.

But if he knew more about dragons than he let on, it might be worth ensuring that our paths did cross again very soon.

Uncertainty clenched my stomach as I crunched through fallen leaves. So vibrant and colorful on tree limbs, but how quickly they became dried husks to be trampled on the ground. I shook my head, trying to dispel the gloomy thought.

Lyuda had been especially mischievous yesterday. She failed to obey my commands twice. Maybe even three times. It was completely reasonable for me to seek out help from the new stable hand.

If the excursion to the quiet paddock took me away from the gossiping noblewomen and guards boasting of their plans to slay the dragons, all the better.

Lukas, our head stable hand for my entire lifetime, waved at my approach. "Your Highness. Weren't you just here yesterday? It's always nice to see a lady take a special interest in her mount."

"Indeed." I straightened my blue riding skirt. "We've had such fair weather lately."

He rose from his bow before I could hurry past. "Can I saddle Lyuda for you?"

"No need. That is…" Warmth coursed up my neck into my cheeks. "I happened to meet the new groom yesterday. Merric, I think his name was? He had some interesting ideas about horse training. I thought perhaps it might be worth trying a new technique with Lyuda. You know, when she doesn't listen."

His sparse brows raised high. "Giving you trouble, is she? I'm happy to help in any way I can, though Merric certainly does have a knack with the animals. Most patient man I've ever seen." He clicked his tongue to the horse he was leading. "Should be around here somewhere."

With a tug on the lead line, he guided the dun horse back toward the stable.

I hurried to keep up. "You do always snatch up the best workers."

He chuckled. "Keep the horses happy, and everyone in the palace benefits."

"I don't doubt it." I slowed my pace, hoping Lukas would follow suit. "And where did you find this newest recruit?"

Lukas scratched at the wide bald spot on the back of his head. "Truth is, he came to us. Seemed quite eager for a job and the horses took to him right away, so I thought I'd give him a chance."

Could he be a spy? I fought back a frown, picturing our former Tsantarian lady's maid. "I wonder what brought him here. Did he say where he's from?"

"No, I don't believe he did." If his narrowed gaze was any indication, my attempt at nonchalance had failed miserably.

But before Lukas could say more, the subject of our conversation strode into view.

"Merric." A commanding tone replaced his fatherly gentleness. "Princess Emelia needs help with her mount. Can you be of assistance?"

"Certainly." Merric hurried forward, pausing partway for a deep bow. "Princess."

"Very good. I'll be nearby, in case you need anything." Lukas darted a glance between the two of us. *Goodness, does the man suspect I have ulterior motives for requesting Merric?* I did, of course, but nothing that should make the wizened man think we needed a chaperone.

I curved my lips into a strained smile. "Thank you, Lukas."

He bowed and backed away.

I scuffed at the ground, the doubts in my mind screaming louder than before. *Why am I here? What will this mysterious stable hand think of me? What should I say to him?*

Merric cleared his throat, breaking the awkward silence. "I believe you were riding Lyuda yesterday? Would you like me to saddle her?"

"Yes, please."

At the tall wooden doors leading into the stables, Merric paused. "You may stay out here, if you prefer. I'm not sure..." He glanced down at the polished boots peeking out from beneath my long skirt.

I shrugged. "I enjoy horses, even if they're a bit messy. I don't mind."

With a nod of approval, he led me inside. Various horses peeked over their stalls to snuffle a greeting.

We reached Lyuda, who had her nose buried in a feed bag. Merric worked with the ease of experience, mumbling softly near her ears as he slipped on her bridle and saddle.

"Here she is." He appeared at the stall door and held out Lyuda's reins. "Did you need anything else?"

Cowardice reared its unease, pressing me to say no. I could abandon this awkward charade, take Lyuda for a ride, and keep what was left of my pride intact.

But I'd learned nothing thus far. Lukas couldn't even tell me where Merric was from, and if I left now, my questions about dragons would forever go unanswered.

Lifting my chin with a confidence I didn't feel, I nodded. "Yes, actually. Lyuda was giving me trouble yesterday. She wouldn't leave off munching on grass when I told her to go forward."

"Hmm, I'll keep an eye out the next few days to make sure she's getting plenty of food." He directed a good-natured smirk my way. "But assuming hunger isn't the problem, then she may just need some reminders on discipline. Horses, especially spirited ones like Lyuda, are likely to take advantage of anyone who's too lax in their commands."

I squinted into the sunshine as we exited the stable. "I have been a bit distracted of late. Perhaps I haven't been firm enough with her."

He shrugged. "It could just as easily be the fault of one or more of the grooms. Lukas trains us well, but even we have our lazy moments."

I widened my eyes in mock horror. "Careful. Lukas might fire you all on the spot if he hears talk like that."

Merric's low chuckle was warm and inviting. I'd so rarely laughed with anyone but my sisters.

He placed a hand on his heart. "I promise to do better in the future. And to make amends for any past transgressions, shall I walk with you and Lyuda to see how she does today?"

"Yes, thank you." I almost hoped my energetic mare would act up, so he'd feel less like he was wasting his time with us.

Merric held out a hand to help me onto Lyuda's back. I tried not to notice how his strong, calloused fingers felt clasping mine. Rougher, but somehow more reassuring and invigorating than the smooth skin of the noblemen who offered their arms or asked me to dance.

"Now, make sure your grip on the reins is firm enough that Lyuda will feel your slightest command, but give her some slack to be comfortable. A discontented animal is likely to act out in all kinds of ways."

I let a bit of the reins slip through my fingers before tightening my grasp.

"Very good." He bowed his head in approval. "You have an impressive riding stance."

I returned his smile, trying not to feel pleased at the compliment. Merric didn't seem the type to give empty flattery, but I was a princess who'd received riding lessons practically since I could walk. That a groom was impressed by my posture shouldn't hold any significance.

He scanned the area, bustling with stable hands hauling tack or leading horses and a few other early-morning riders setting off on the trails. "It looks like the southern pasture is open. Should we head there?"

I nodded and spurred Lyuda into a slow walk, allowing Merric to keep up at her side.

He gave a few more tips along the way, then talked us through some simple exercises. Lyuda—fickle creature—decided to be on her best behavior, but Merric worked with us as patiently as though she were new to the stables or returning from an injury.

I pulled Lyuda to a stop at the far end of the fencing, where Merric watched as we completed a series of alternating speeds and directions.

"Well, I'm not seeing any trouble today." He shaded his eyes as he looked up at me. "No doubt she can tell we're onto her tricks."

I laughed and gave Lyuda a pat. "That sounds like this smart girl."

"But I'm always happy to help if something shows up again." Merric raised a hand, as though preparing to depart.

"Thank you for taking the time to work with us this morning." My words tripped over each other in a rush to keep him engaged. "Have you always worked with horses?"

He ran a hand through his hair, better combed today in the absence of his hat. "Animals of various kinds. I often find them easier to understand than people."

"I know what you mean." Our gazes met with a level of understanding that didn't seem possible in our short acquaintance. But I couldn't afford to be distracted—not when this private time with him was coming to an end. "I believe you mentioned seeing dragons in your previous travels. Did you work with them at all?"

His laugh held a nervous edge. "I don't think anyone works with dragons in the way one works with horses. Their intelligence and ability to communicate is so much greater..." He ducked his head, shifting his feet. "At least, I imagine they'd be much harder to control."

I swallowed, thinking through my next statement. "But don't they sometimes do people's bidding? I've heard that people even ride them."

He rubbed the back of his neck. "If a dragon is ridden by a person, it seems like it'd be more of an equal partnership than a rider and mount. And such a magnificent creature could hardly be controlled by a bridle and reins."

Equal partnership. I choked back a bitter laugh. "Not by bridle and reins, true. But by words, perhaps? When spoken in their language? What did you call it yesterday...*CxIyVhAuNz*?"

He shook his head, his guarded expression turning to a frown. "I'd hardly know, Princess. And I wouldn't recommend meddling in such things."

"But if dragons ever became a threat to Oneska—"

"I am a mere stable hand, Your Highness. Surely the guards would be more appropriate to consult in such a situation." He bowed, polite but stiff. "Let me know if you have any further trouble with Lyuda. In the meantime, I'd best get back."

"Of course. Thank you." The rote words left my mouth without conscious thought. I watched him go, my mind a blur of questions.

Was he truly as inexperienced with dragons as he claimed? Then what was it about the subject that had closed off our easy camaraderie?

CHAPTER 5

GOLDEN SCALES REFLECTED IN the waning sunlight angling through the library window.

Oh no. My book—a treatise on large reptiles—clattered to the floor.

After my conversation with Merric had ended on such a disappointing note days before, I'd done what research I could on dragons. A difficult task when our vast library didn't seem to hold a single tome devoted to the topic.

But when nearly a week had passed without any sign of the Tsantarian monsters, a trace of hope had stirred in my chest. Despite Prince Leonnar's terse dismissal of my concerns, perhaps our last conversation had left an impression after all.

Apparently, a lengthy reprieve had been too much to hope for.

With a sigh, I rose from the leather armchair I'd been nestled in and picked up the book. I replaced it on the shelf, running my fingers along the worn spines of its neighbors. But even the scent and feel of books couldn't lift my spirits.

A closer look out the window revealed the entire set of five dragons taking a second pass around the palace. Poor Jolene was likely fighting back tears if she'd seen them already. And Father...

I froze mid-step. Would anyone try something to scare off or injure the dragons tonight?

What if it worked? Cautious hope swirled with dread in my stomach, sending bile up my throat. Would I or one of my sisters be forced to marry a complete stranger?

Or, more likely, what if it angered the beasts? Dread of an entirely different kind made me shiver. Did they have any level of restraint? Or would they burn down the palace, as Prince Leonnar had threatened so many times?

I hurried down the corridor, my slippers swishing against the red-tinged granite. My confused maid had ordered me another pair just this week, marveling at how quickly I wore them out.

If only she knew the half of it.

Rosalind burst from the music room, Pippa at her heels. Rose hurried forward to meet me, scanning the hall in either direction. She tugged at her skirts, her perfect features pinched into a frown. "You saw them, too?"

"I'm afraid so."

Pippa bounced on her toes. "I'll finally get to dance tonight!" The rest of us had attended a ball hosted by Duke Virkalt the evening before, and Pippa had bemoaned the woes of being too young all morning.

"Perhaps, but keep your voice down." An undertone of fear dampened Rose's usual confidence. "I do hope Eugen was bluffing when he said he'd handle the dragons the next time they make an appearance. Not that I'd mind marrying him, if it came to that, but it's more likely he..." She clutched my arm, letting her words trail off.

I patted her hand. "I know he admires you very much, but hopefully being faced with the dragons up close will inspire caution."

She nodded, her jaw tight.

"You wouldn't marry Eugen, would you?" Pippa skipped along beside us. "His laugh sounds like a barking dog."

Rose's sparkling giggle echoed through the hall. "Very true. I can do better."

I nudged Pippa. "You mustn't say such unkind things. At least, not so loudly."

She shrugged, unperturbed. "Danil has a much nicer laugh. Like a true gentleman."

Rose's arm tightened, all traces of humor gone.

I glanced down the corridor again, only spotting a guard far ahead. "There's nothing gentlemanly about dragging princesses away from their home in the middle of the night, Pippa."

Her nose wrinkled. "It's not Danil's fault that Leonnar's so bossy."

I almost laughed at the blunt description of the Tsantarian Crown Prince. "You're right. But you should still be cautious about—"

"There you are." Calli darted toward us from the wing of the palace that held our chambers, her smile lacking its usual exuberance. "We should go to Father. I heard a cry when the dragons first came into view. Perhaps it wasn't him, but I fear he won't take their reappearance well."

"He never does," muttered Rosalind.

I squeezed Calli's shoulder with my free hand. "Hopefully we can calm him down at dinner."

"And Jolene." Pippa peeked out every window we passed, as though making sure the dragons hadn't changed their minds and headed back to Tsantar. *If only.* "Good thing she wasn't in the music room this time, or she might've snapped another harp string."

Scrambling up Indigo's back had never before brought a sense of relief. But although the dragons had made Father and everyone around him as tense as ever, nothing out of the ordinary had occurred. I'd strained my ears the entire evening for some kind of shout or ruckus, but all had remained quiet. Perhaps we'd overreacted, and the gentlemen who might've been tempted by Father's challenge were too intimidated by the dragons to act on it.

Now we just needed to make it away from the palace. How ironic, to feel that for once Tsantar would be a place of relative safety.

I twisted, squinting through the darkness to see Pippa climbing onto Scarlet's back. As though waiting for the same signal, my dragon stretched its wings and lifted off from the tower. I ducked, clinging tight as it rose higher.

"They're getting away!" The cry came from far below.

I froze. Why would someone object to the dragons leaving? Unless... *Faster, Indigo.* But what about my sisters? I tried to look back for them, but the dragon's breadth blocked my view.

"Not this time." The gruff warning resonated along the cobblestone streets of the royal city that expanded in all directions beyond the palace grounds.

No, no, no. Not while we're on their backs!

The air hummed as a thick bolt from a crossbow sailed past. A scream from somewhere nearby mixed with yells and shouts below.

Was that Rosalind?

A guttural roar drowned out every other sound, setting my nerves on edge. Presumably, a dragon had been hit. But which one? And was it injured? Was Rose hurt? Scenes of my sisters pierced by arrows or catapulting to the ground played through my mind, each more horrific than the one before.

My dragon lurched as another projectile whizzed past. It didn't seem to hit any of its targets, but that brought little comfort. Surely if they planned to take out the entire set of dragons, they had plenty—

More screams erupted from the crowd, along with a roar of a different kind. Light blazed on the far side of the square, growing too bright too fast for such a dark night.

Fire. My gaze darted frantically over the scene of running people and billowing smoke. I tried to orient myself in my shifting aerial view. Wasn't the bakery on that corner of the thoroughfare before it curved toward the fountain? My heart constricted as I pictured the plump, gentle baker and his no-nonsense wife.

How many more people would suffer because of Father's hasty proclamation? Because of Prince Leonnar's threats and greed?

I tensed for another attack, but the focus of the people below had shifted to subduing the flames eating at the baker's home and shop. And despite angry grunts and huffs, the dragons seemed to be moving away. I dared to raise my head high enough to get a better view. All five dragons still soared through the air, and none seemed to be missing a rider.

An exhaled part-sigh, part-sob constricted my chest as I drooped back against my dragon's neck.

The ride felt agonizingly long. I periodically sat up and searched the darkness for signs of any injury to my sisters, only to press my forehead to Indigo's scales in frustration when I couldn't see anything useful. My tight muscles trembled with fatigue by the time tangy salt scented the air, and we began our descent.

I half leaped, half fell from my dragon's back the moment its feet touched the balcony.

The other beasts alighted one by one. I ran for Rose's green mount, squinting for signs of blood. "Rose? Rose, are you hurt? Was your dragon the one who started the fire?"

She slid down, shaking chestnut curls from her face. "I'm fine, no thanks to that ignoramus who shot at us." She fluffed her skirts in a tiff, as though it had been meant as a personal offense. "The arrow bounced off Emerald's scales as though a child had tossed a toy. I doubt it even made a scratch."

I flung my arms around her. "But it didn't touch you? I was so worried."

She huffed a laugh, giving me a quick squeeze before stepping back. "No harm done, Em. Truly. To either of us." She gave her dragon a rueful glance. "In all honesty, the flame was more frightening than whatever the villagers were launching."

"How dreadful! Did it burn you?"

"Did you see who shot the arrow?"

"Was your dragon hurt or just mad?"

Calli, Jo, and Pippa surrounded us, peppering Rose with questions.

Prince Leonnar's voice cut through the cacophony. "Princesses of Oneska, welcome."

We fell silent, turning to face him. *Should we tell him?* He no doubt suspected something was amiss based on our unusual behavior. Did the dragons have a way to communicate the details of the attack?

His brows furrowed in mock concern. "Is something wrong? Surely you young ladies didn't come all this way just to chat with each other. But you seem distraught."

As though he cared whether any of his actions caused us distress. My internal debate raged faster. What could we say that was honest but wouldn't anger him?

Pippa jumped forward before any of us could stop her. "Someone aimed an arrow at Rose's dragon! And her dragon got mad and shot fire right out of its mouth." Her wide eyes held a mix of horror and excitement.

Calli put a hand on her shoulder, but the damage had been done.

"Shot at *WdOeFlCx*?" He turned to the dragon, whose green scales shone in the torchlight emanating from inside the citadel. "He is unhurt, I presume?"

"We aren't aware of any injury." I'd have to answer his questions quickly if I wanted to keep Pippa out of the conversation.

"Hmm. *VhIyBrQk AuNz.*" He tipped his head toward the dragon.

Emerald Scales gave his wings a flick. "*BrIyGt.*" The low, guttural tone sounded ancient, other-worldly.

Prince Leonnar nodded, apparently satisfied by the reply. "And fair Rosalind?" He gestured to Rose. "I sincerely hope your fellow countryman's foolish actions didn't cause you harm."

Rose squared her shoulders. "None whatsoever."

"Excellent." He patted the emerald dragon's leg, then issued a command. *IyFlOeWd?* The dragons huffed and took off from the balcony, swooping around toward the southern end of the citadel grounds.

Prince Leonnar watched them go, then faced us once more. "What an exciting evening you ladies have had already. I'm very grateful no one was hurt in the incident."

Except those whose home and livelihood were consumed by fire. I winced as the sight returned to my mind's eye. So much destruction. An entire building, gone in a matter of minutes. Had they contained the fire to only the bakery? Or had it spread beyond?

Beside me, Jolene trembled. I put an arm around her waist.

"But it does beg the question, why would anyone do such a thing? Did my dragons do something to incite their wrath?" Prince Leonnar's gaze found mine, more threatening than concerned.

I swallowed, the taste of smoke lingering in my dry mouth. "Nothing out of the ordinary, no. But as I mentioned before, their continued presence in Oneska is starting to cause alarm..."

"Ah, that." He flicked his hand, as though dislodging a pesky fly. "How disappointing that you weren't able to quell your kingdom's concerns before things got out of hand in this way. You know, the citizens of Philistra had similar fears about the Tsantarian dragons before... Well, I'd hate for our friendly visits to be marred by such ugliness." With a fake smile, he motioned us into the citadel. "Come, let's join the festivities."

My sisters preceded us, sending nervous glances our way.

Once they were a few steps ahead, Prince Leonnar leaned close. "I trust you won't make the same mistake again."

CHAPTER 6

I rubbed my eyes, stifling a yawn.

Calli put an arm around my shoulders. She'd tiptoed out of our chamber behind me, cautious not to wake our sleeping sisters. "You must let yourself get some rest, Em." She leaned her head against my arm and lowered her voice. "This isn't your burden to bear alone."

"I did sleep." A second poorly-timed yawn didn't bolster my claim.

Calli gave me her best attempt at a stern frown.

"A little, at least." I sighed and massaged my aching forehead. "But how many more people will get hurt? How many more livelihoods destroyed?" I blinked back the tears welling in my bleary eyes. "How long until those creatures kill someone? It will be on my hands if I don't at least try to stop them."

"None of this is your fault." Calli paused until I met her gaze. "You can't possibly blame yourself for Prince Leonnar's actions."

"Of course I don't." Though perhaps if I'd suspected the Tsantarian lady's maid who'd fooled us all… I shook away the unhelpful thought. "But you know I feel responsible for all of you. And Father wants to help, but he's in no position to truly—"

"I know." She steered me farther down the corridor as I swiped at my eyes. "But now he may finally be willing to listen to reason. I'm not sure he realized the true danger before. If he calls off this contest, then the situation will no longer be so urgent."

"I hope you're right." I closed my eyes and heaved a fortifying breath, then opened the door to the breakfast room.

Father was already there, his plate nearly empty. Fresh pain stabbed at my chest at the sight of the deep purple hollows beneath his eyes.

"Good morning, Father." Calli's voice radiated her usual optimism and cheer.

"Good morning, girls." His lips barely tipped into a dim smile.

I claimed the chair beside him without bothering to get any food and clasped his free hand. "Have you heard any updates about the baker and his wife? Will they be all right? Are the guards helping to rebuild their shop?"

His arm tensed. "How do you know about that business with the bakery? You and your sisters should've been asleep long before—"

"We could hardly sleep through such a ruckus, Father." Calli gently interrupted him, giving me a warning look. She sat across from us, her plate holding a blueberry muffin and several slices of candy melon. "Once we saw the flames, we couldn't help but be concerned."

"What could've angered that dragon, do you think?" I had to concede Calli had a point—Father might get suspicious if I revealed I knew too much.

"Sir Tarant shot a volley of arrows at it, thinking to hide under cover of darkness." His chest puffed out. "A valiant attempt to end the creature."

Calli and I exchanged a worried glance before she turned her focus back to Father. "Very brave, certainly. But do you think it even did any damage? The dragons' scales seem to be so strong."

"We won't know unless we keep trying." Father shoveled a forkful of potatoes into his mouth.

Keep trying? Dread twisted my insides, making me even less hungry than before. "But Father, surely we can't let incidents like this continue. We don't have the resources to rebuild every shop in the Gryfadele. And if people get hurt, or killed, by the dragons' wrath—"

"They must be exterminated." He trembled, making his chair clatter. "We can't back down now. The battle for Oneska has begun, and we must redouble our efforts if we're to drive this curse from our land."

"Perhaps we should wait, though." The Maker only knew how Calli was still managing to smile. "Deceive them into thinking we've given up? An element of surprise might be to our benefit."

Father raised his glass toward her before downing the rest of his juice. "An interesting thought. I shall discuss it with the captain."

Well done, Calli. My racing pulse slowed a notch. "Have you heard anything of the baker and his wife? Did they survive the attack?"

Father nodded, his expression grave but no longer frantic. "Indeed. In need of some fresh air and bandages, but the healers seemed to think they could set them to rights."

"I'm so glad to hear it."

I wandered to the sideboard as Calli made suggestions for how the baker might serve in our own kitchens until his shop was reestablished. My tired mind continued to process Father's reaction as I piled strawberries next to a slice of toast on my plate. Even if he agreed to pause attacks against the dragons, he clearly had no intention of stopping, no matter how many innocent people were hurt in the process.

The responsibility to bring this to an end still landed squarely on my shoulders.

Father rose from the table as I returned to my seat. "Enjoy your breakfast. I must meet with Captain Venedict without delay." He paused on his way to the door. His face held more warmth and less anger than I'd seen in months. "I know you must be frightened, my dear ones. But know that I will stop at nothing to make our kingdom safe for you again." Raising a fist in the Oneskan sign of support and solidarity, he squared his shoulders and left the room.

I raised a shaking fist, blinking back more tears. His intentions were so good, but his unwillingness to abandon this plan could lead to our ruin.

Calli watched me as I returned to my plate. "At least he's considering a pause in the attacks."

"That is something." I popped a few berries into my mouth, their fresh, sweet taste nearly lost on me. "But if last night didn't convince him to call this whole thing off, I don't know what will."

"He wants the same outcome we do. Maybe one of his knights really will find a way to—"

"I'm going to the stables." I polished off my toast in two bites.

"The stables?" Calli's fork remained suspended halfway between her plate and her mouth. "This early in the morning?"

"I need some fresh air." And to have a talk with a certain handsome stable hand who I could only hope would be less evasive after the events of last evening.

"That does sound refreshing. I think I'll join you." She picked up the remainder of her muffin and replaced her napkin on the table.

"Oh. Well, I..."

"Join you where?" Pippa appeared in the doorway, all restless curiosity.

"We're going for a ride. You're welcome to come too." Calli had apparently taken over this outing and was intent on steering it in the opposite direction of my plans.

Pippa nodded. "Do you think they'll let me ride Natasa again?" She darted to the sideboard to snatch a muffin.

"I don't see why not. You did very well with her last time."

I suppressed a groan. So much for a private talk with Merric.

"Princess Emelia." Merric sounded surprised, but not displeased, to see me as we neared the stable yard. He set aside the bag of feed he'd been hauling and opened his mouth to go on, but his gaze landed on my sisters trailing behind. "Ah, and…"

"You remember my sister, Princess Callista."

Calli gave him a warm smile as he bowed toward her.

"And this is our youngest sister, Princess Pippa."

Pippa's brows furrowed as Merric bowed again. "Who are you?"

Calli jumped in before Merric or I could respond. "This is Merric, a new stable hand at the palace."

"Oh." Pippa shrugged. "Can I ride Natasa?"

Merric's lips twisted in half-concern, half-amusement. "I…" He glanced at me, and I gave a quick nod. "I believe you may. Let's go see if she's available to be saddled."

I joined Merric as he reclaimed the feed bag and led the way into the stables. Behind us, Calli gave Pippa a gentle lecture about proper introduction etiquette.

Merric held the door open for me. "Has Lyuda given you any further trouble? We've been running her through some paces each day, and she seems to be obeying well."

Hopefully the sudden darkness of the stable hid the pink that was likely coloring my cheeks. "That's good to hear. She must've just needed a little reminder."

"Sometimes that's all it takes, along with consistency. I'm assuming you'd like to ride her today? You can let me know if she falls back into any bad habits." He grabbed a bridle and saddle and motioned to another stable hand.

Calli stepped closer with a frown. "You didn't mention Lyuda's been giving you trouble."

Merric glanced back at me, his expression curious. *If only one of the horses would make a commotion right about now.*

"It wasn't anything to concern you with. You know how headstrong she can be. Merric gave me some pointers, and she's improved already."

"I'm glad to hear it." Calli's smile was too eager as she looked between us. "Perhaps Merric should join us today, in case Lyuda needs any further instruction."

Pippa scrutinized the stable hand. "Would you let me ride fast? My sisters never do."

Merric chuckled. "Maybe across an open meadow. We could take the path that leads through the western corner of the forest past the lake."

"Huzzah!" Pippa skipped down the row and around the corner to where her new favorite horse was housed. The other stable hand followed her.

The rest of us paused in front of Lyuda's stall.

I patted her glossy dark neck, drawing reassurance from her warmth, before daring a glance at Merric. "Thank you, but please don't feel obligated. I'm sure you have plenty of work to do here, and Lyuda really hasn't been too bad..."

He tipped his head close. "Do you object to me going? I'm happy to help, but I certainly don't want to impose on your time with your sisters."

"I don't object at all!" *That sounded too enthusiastic.* With a final pat to Lyuda's forehead, I faced Merric. "That is, we would enjoy your company if you can spare the time."

"It would be my honor." Why did those golden-green eyes make my stomach do strange flips? "No work around here could be as important as escorting three lovely princesses. And it will provide a good opportunity to see how our new stallion handles riding in a group."

"Thank you." I stepped aside so he could saddle Lyuda, wishing I could bury myself in a stack of hay. I conversed easily with nobles and foreign royalty all the time. Why did a stable hand who happened to be attractive make me so flustered?

Pippa squealed with delight as Natasa cantered across the meadow, the white spots on her coat blurring as she picked up speed.

Calli laughed and followed, flashing me a knowing smile I didn't appreciate.

What, exactly, does she think she knows?

Our conversation had been formal, stilted, thus far on our ride. The weather, the trails, the horses, Merric's experiences during his time in our kingdom. As usual, he deftly avoided sharing any details about his family or past.

His chestnut stallion, Kirill, leaned his head forward, and Merric tugged the reins. "No, boy. It's not your turn to run. It wouldn't do to leave Princess Emelia behind."

"Oh, thank you. But we can..."

Merric shook his head. "No need. It's good practice for him to learn some restraint." He leaned down to give his horse a quiet command, then turned toward me. "It's a pleasure to see your sister enjoying herself so much."

"You'll be a favorite of hers from now on." I shook my head as Pippa issued another triumphant cry far ahead. "She's a sweet girl, though she could afford to learn some restraint herself."

He chuckled. "That will come with time. For now, let her enjoy being young, free from responsibilities."

I nodded, dropping my gaze. The very thought brought mist to my eyes. Though less than ten years Pippa's senior, I felt as though responsibilities had pressed upon me for my entire life.

Merric brought Kirill around to face me. "You, on the other hand, seem even more burdened with responsibilities than usual, Princess Emelia. Lyuda has behaved well, from what I've seen, but if there's anything I can do to help..."

His tight-lipped smile belied his relaxed shrug. Clearly, he could tell that my problems had nothing to do with my horse. Most people were too busy bowing or pandering to wonder what worries accompanied my coveted royal status. Merric's insightfulness unnerved me. Yet he tread carefully, respecting my privacy.

Why was he so much harder to ignore than all the titled gentlemen who'd been paraded before me for years?

"I hardly know if you could help. If anyone could help..." But I had to try. "Did you hear of the tragedy at the bakery last evening?"

He kept the smile on his face, but his eyes turned guarded. "Something about a fire?"

I scoffed, my irritation making Lyuda dance to the side. "No ordinary fire. The dragons swarmed the castle again last night. Someone shot an arrow at one of them, and in retaliation—"

"Why would someone shoot at them?"

I started at the intensity of his question. "I know you're fairly new to Kavalya Palace. These dragons have been a menace for months. Every few nights they appear around dusk and circle the towers." I swallowed, uncertain how much to share. "Everyone finds them unsettling, not understanding their intentions. My father is desperate to be rid of them. So much so that he's offered...a reward."

Merric rubbed the back of his neck. "Ah, yes. The successful claimant would become a prince, I believe? Through marriage."

Heat seared my cheeks. Why had I wanted a private conversation with this man today? "Precisely." I muttered the word through clenched teeth, unable to meet his gaze.

He cleared his throat. "So whoever shot at the dragons was rising to your father's challenge."

"We can only assume." Embarrassment mixed with my anxiety, churning my insides.

He nodded, lips pressed together in thought. "But you seek to solve the dilemma yourself."

"Yes." I dared to look up. Those unusual eyes studied me, but I couldn't tell what he was looking for.

He blinked and shook his head. "Have these dragons done any harm?"

Air huffed through my nose. Clearly, I was spending too much time around the vile creatures. "Only threatened it, until last night."

"I see." He clenched his fingers in Kirill's mane. "Well, I doubt..."

In the distance, Pippa let out a whoop. Hoof beats thundered in our direction. *I'm running out of time.*

"Merric." I grasped his arm before I could pause to think. "I know you said your experience with dragons is limited, but if you have any information that would be helpful to us... I want to put an end to this before someone gets hurt."

He closed his eyes, lines creasing his temples. "That would be my hope as well." He squeezed my hand, letting his fingertips linger over mine. "You don't know why they've chosen Kavalya Palace?"

I opened my mouth, then closed it. "I don't... That is, they seem to be a warning from a neighboring kingdom." The truth danced on my tongue, but I couldn't risk divulging it to someone I'd known for such a short time.

"Hmm." He studied me with a frown. As though he knew I was being just as evasive as he always was around this subject. His gaze traveled to where Pippa and Calli approached, the wind whipping their hair back from their laughing faces. He leaned close, releasing his hold. "I'll see if there's anything I can do."

"Thank you." I pulled back my hand, hope stuttering in my chest. Was there truly something he could do to help?

If so, would he want to marry one of us?

Chapter 7

"Purple is my favorite color on you." Calli helped pull a beautiful gown of deep violet over my head.

The dragons had appeared again at dinnertime, just three days after the attack. I'd been nearly as distracted as Father, glancing out every window and unable to concentrate on a given task all evening. But my jittery pulse had begun to slow when we reached our feigned bedtime preparations with no obvious attempts at scaring or injuring the creatures.

Hopefully any potential dragon slayers had been cowed by the first disastrous attempt.

Calli leaned close as my head reappeared from the frothy layers of material, lowering her voice. "If only you were heading to the stables instead of Tsantar."

"The stables?" My voice squeaked, as nervous energy of a new kind thrummed through my veins.

I busied myself straightening the bodice of my dress. "I suppose I'd rather go anywhere than Tsantar, but it would be an odd time of night to ride a horse."

She shrugged, adjusting the beaded neckline of my collar. "Perhaps. But I imagine a certain handsome stable hand would appreciate seeing you in this dress."

My gaze flew to our younger sisters, who were engrossed in their own chatter and preparations. "Lukas is far too old for me." The whisper came out tighter than I'd hoped.

Calli's amused gaze met mine. "Merric, however, is not."

I imitated one of Rose's dramatic sighs. "If any of the stable hands were to see me in this gown, they would likely think I'm ridiculous and get back to work."

She clicked her tongue. "I saw the way the two of you were talking the other day. You've rarely given such focus to any other gentleman. And he's smart, courteous, intriguing, handsome—"

"You already mentioned that he's handsome." I raised a brow. "You haven't tired of poor Duke Virkalt already, have you?"

"Of course not." She gave me the closest thing to a scolding look she was capable of. "Besides, Merric doesn't watch me the way he watches you."

"He's been helping me with Lyuda, remember? No doubt he's looking for flaws in my horsemanship." If my heart skipped a beat at her statement, it was only anxiety about the coming dragon ride.

"If you say so." She deftly swept my hair into a simple chignon, leaving one curl dangling free. "But don't discount him just because he's a stable hand."

"Romance is the furthest thing from my mind right now, Calli. If Merric can't help us with the dragon situation, I have no interest in him." I sat on my bed to tie on my dancing slippers, perhaps yanking the laces harder than necessary.

"And if he can help?"

I sensed her watching me, but I refused to look up.

"Calli, I did the buttons wrong again." Pippa's wail saved me from further scrutiny.

My hands clenched tighter than ever as I climbed to the top of our tower. Father had agreed with Calli's idea of spreading out the attacks to maintain an element of surprise, but had all the guards agreed with the plan? Or would someone else entirely make an attempt tonight?

I tried to take a deep breath, but my chest remained as constricted as though my stays had been laced directly to my ribcage. Our visits to Tsantar were stressful enough before we'd become the targets of sharp, flying projectiles.

Calli and Rose took my hands once we reached the top, joining Pippa and Jo to each end of our united line. Apparently, I wasn't the only one who needed extra comfort this evening. I'd do anything to spare my sisters from this situation, but at the moment I was grateful not to be alone.

We mounted our dragons quickly, the silence below almost eerie. No doubt everyone was asleep or closed in for the night, perhaps hiding away from the dragons. *Or lying in wait.* I dismissed the disturbing thought and gripped Indigo's scales as it lifted off the roof.

Our flight seemed filled with rustling sounds and creaking. A combination of my heightened senses and crisp leaves vibrating on dry branches. Despite my very reasonable explanation, I couldn't help looking around every other minute, even after we'd left Kavalya Palace far behind.

Only Pippa, in back, seemed to share my paranoia. The few times I glimpsed her, she'd craned her neck to glance behind. She was so young, it was no surprise that even her sunny confidence had been dampened by the attack.

Next time, I'll see if I can get Indigo Scales to fly last in line.

Prince Leonnar oozed his usual false charm as we left our dragons and lined up to enter the citadel. Pippa still searched the darkness beyond the balcony, her thin brows furrowed. *She really must think something's out there if even the prospect of seeing Danil hasn't distracted her.* I moved in her direction, but Calli was there first, taking Pippa's arm and fluffing her sleeve.

With one last glance behind, I let Leonnar lead me inside.

"Young Pippa seems a bit preoccupied this evening." His deceptively friendly tone held an undercurrent of warning. "I do hope there was no further unpleasantness among your knights or commonfolk this evening."

At least that I could answer honestly. "No, we had a peaceful journey." My smile was as genuine as he'd ever received. "But I think we were all a bit rattled last time, and Pippa is at such an impressionable age."

"True." His lips curled into a predatory smile. "No doubt her time with Danil will offer some comfort and peace of mind."

I barely held back a grunt. The last thing we needed was for Danil to play a hero, though Pippa was hardly a damsel in distress. "It's kind of you to be concerned. No doubt she'll recover quickly."

"I do hope so."

Faint music drifted up the spiral stairway. He likely wouldn't reveal anything, but... "Speaking of recovery, did you find any injury on your dragon the other night? The one with green scales?"

His chuckle was short, flippant. "Certainly not. Though it's kind of you to be concerned."

His sarcastic repetition of my own words wasn't lost on me. *Why must I spend night after night in this odious man's presence?* But I wouldn't let his pettiness thwart my purpose. "Are their scales truly impenetrable, then?"

Leonnar puffed out his chest. "Better protection than the finest armor."

"How fortunate for them." A touch of bitterness seeped into my tone. I took a deep breath and widened my eyes, aiming for naivete. "But how is it that such powerful creatures, with seemingly no weaknesses, would allow themselves to be controlled by humans?"

He paused a short way from the ballroom doors, halting my steps. "Ah, my dear Emelia." He tapped a finger to the tip of my nose. "I thought you already knew the rules. If you want to be privy to the secrets of my kingdom, you must first willingly marry me."

Matvey burst through the door, freeing me from the need to respond. "Rosalind, there you are. I thought I heard Leonnar's voice and hoped you'd be along."

"Of course." Rosalind darted a concerned glance my way before flouncing toward him. "Your brother always finds us."

Matvey lowered a brow. "Perhaps I ought to be the one to meet the dragons next time."

Leonnar sent him a look filled with...anger? Warning? "You know they behave best when I handle them."

Matvey reddened. "Well, I—"

Rosalind looped her arm with his, donning her brightest smile. "What is a little walk down the stairs compared with the night of dancing we have ahead of us? Let's not miss the party by loitering out here in the drafty hall."

"Certainly, Princess Rosalind." Matvey nodded and hurried forward.

Jolene rolled her eyes, and even Calli looked amused as the rest of us shuffled into the ballroom. I almost felt sorry for Matvey, picturing the droves of suitors waiting for Rose in Oneska.

The ballroom was bedecked in its usual vibrant array of colors. Guests laughed, danced, and took refreshments passed around by harried servants. I shook my head, trying to clear the feeling of a nightmare on endless repeat. Slight changes in guests or music or decor, but always the same forced discussion with the man who sought to control me and my kingdom. Always the same dance.

No, something will change. We'll find a way to make it change. Hopefully for the better.

Leonnar led me through a number of dances, then introduced me to a nobleman who rarely visited. I played my part, knowing Leonnar would cut me off before I spoke more than a few words. My role was to be seen—paraded about—never heard.

"You promised me a dance, Leonnar." A courtier with a red gown hugging her frame and long, blond curls placed a hand on the Crown Prince's shoulder. She smiled at Leonnar before frowning at me.

I nodded to her, fighting a laugh. She was more than welcome to steal him away. *Forever, with any luck.*

"That I did. Please, excuse me." Leonnar bowed to us and followed her to the center of the floor.

With Leonnar otherwise occupied, could I say something to this nobleman? To someone else? Surely not everyone in this room would condone the royal family's behavior if they knew the truth. But already I could feel Leonnar's eyes on me. And how could I know who would turn out to be friend versus foe?

I gave the nobleman a polite smile and walked away. Help was unlikely to be found among any ally of Tsantar.

Pippa approached, looking surprisingly excited considering she was sitting this dance out to give Jolene a turn. "Em!" She sidled close, her eyes almost comically wide. "I saw someone."

I lowered my brows. "There are a lot of *someones* here tonight, as usual. The Tsantarian royal family seems incapable of hosting a small event."

She shook her head. "That's not what I mean. Someone we know."

I stiffened, trying to keep the panic off my face. "Someone who's visited Kavalya Palace is now a guest here?" I scanned every nearby face, but my thoughts jumbled too quickly to make sense of what I was seeing.

Was the truth of our nighttime ventures about to be discovered and reported to Father?

"No, not a guest." She rolled her eyes and leaned closer. "He's hiding."

"A gentleman we know is hiding here?" My pulse slowed a notch. Perhaps the fear surrounding our departure was playing tricks with Pippa's mind.

"I saw him under a table. By the door." She inclined her head in a way that was clearly meant to be subtle.

"Ah, how mysterious." I struggled to maintain a serious tone. "What did he look like?"

Pippa sighed. "Like I said, we know him."

"Yes, but who—"

"That groom from the stables who went riding with us. Wearing the hat." She patted the top of her head.

The hat? *Merric.* My amusement fled, replaced by terror. He'd said he would try to help...what if he actually was here? "But how would he get here?" The question was as much for myself as Pippa.

"I don't know, but I kept hearing sounds behind us as we flew here tonight. I bet it was him." She placed her hands on her hips, as though that settled the matter.

But my bewilderment only grew. Could he follow us here? How could he keep up with dragons? And if he were here now, then what? He could get caught, or cause a disruption, or tell Father, or...

Leonnar appeared before me. "Ready for our next dance, Princess Emelia?"

I straightened, taking a deep breath. If Merric truly had gotten himself inside Yrtulk Citadel somehow, I couldn't afford a single misstep. "Of course."

He led me toward the center of the ballroom as the string players plucked out the staccato opening notes of a rovodan. I swallowed a sigh. Oneskan dances were graceful and flowing, while Tsantarian dances were filled with jumps and sharp, precise movements. The rovodan was exhausting, but at least it wouldn't allow for much conversation.

Leonnar linked his arm with mine as we spun in alternate directions. I tapped my foot, hopped, then tapped again in quick succession. Every time we faced away from each other, I scanned the room, carefully keeping my head steady and returning my gaze to Leonnar whenever I spun into his view.

The cycles of the dance brought us closer to the door Pippa had indicated, and my pulse thrummed in my ears. Surely, I'd only imagined the tablecloth shifting beneath a large spread of tea and desserts.

I returned my gaze to the spot with every spin. When the musicians slowed for the final chords of the piece, I winced. Of course no one was hiding under the table. Pippa's imagination simply...

Then the gauzy silver fabric slipped aside, and a face appeared next to the table leg. *Merric.* Our gazes locked, his intense but unreadable. Then the curtain of the tablecloth swung back into place, and he was gone.

How did he get here? And what did he hope to accomplish?

I forced a tight smile in response to Leonnar's chatter about some foreign diplomat they were hosting. *Breathe, Emelia. Act normal.*

"Shall we ask a servant to get you a dessert? As you can see, this evening's selection is excellent." Leonnar gestured toward the very table I wanted to avoid.

"Dessert?" The word came out as a half-squeak. I cleared my throat, attempting a laugh. "I'm sure it's delicious, but I'm much too full. Shouldn't we dance again?"

He raised his brows at my rare enthusiasm. "If you'd like."

We joined the end of a line of dancers jumping with their right knees raised. Ignoring my tired feet, I focused on the steps, the music, Leonnar's occasional commentary.

Anything but the table concealing our enigmatic, golden-eyed stable hand.

CHAPTER 8

"Merric?" The inquiry came out as a soft growl. A swirl of anger, fear, and hope had kept me awake most of the night after returning to the palace beneath a sky sprinkled with stars. I circled the stable yard, half wanting to leave and pretend I hadn't spotted Merric at the ball, half wanting to shout until he appeared.

He'd gotten an opportunity to see me in my purple gown last night after all, just like Calli wanted. But why? And how?

No movement or sound broke the morning stillness, aside from twittering sparrows and shifting horses. I peered at each paddock, squinting to see the farthest wooden fences. "Merric?"

Where is everyone? Perhaps I'd come too early, or they utilized a more distant training yard. But if Merric wasn't here, how else would I track him down? Had he even made it back from Tsantar? I flushed at the thought of asking around the stables for him. No doubt Lukas would be more suspicious than ever. Perhaps he...

"Princess Emelia." Merric led a tall, chestnut stallion from the direction of the pasture, the same one he'd brought on our ride with

Calli and Pippa. "I thought I heard someone, but I didn't realize…" Something more than surprise laced his tone. Caution? Guilt?

"I've been looking for you." With no one else around, I didn't bother to pretend I was at the stables for any other purpose.

"Ah. Aren't I a lucky one?" His smile seemed almost sardonic, with no trace of its former impish charm. "My apologies for my absence, I hope you haven't been waiting long. Kirill here took some convincing to leave his food trough." The stallion snuffled at his fingers as Merric stroked his neck.

Lucky, indeed. The anger and dread simmering in my veins thrummed for release. But I couldn't afford to scare him away before he answered my questions, so I kept my tone neutral. "I'm afraid I must interrupt your work. Can you suggest somewhere we can talk without being overheard?"

"Certainly." His ruddy cheeks paled as he tightened his grip on the horse's bridle, then dipped into a hasty bow. He glanced around the yard, his gaze lingering on the broad doors of the stable. "Follow me."

Please, don't let anyone be out on a ride yet this morning. My tete-a-tete with a handsome young stable hand would be sure to get tongues wagging.

He led the way through a gate, past an open pasture, and onto a wooded trail. I kept my pace measured, my feet moving painfully slowly compared with my racing mind. Kirill seemed just as impatient with our measured strides, tossing his head and nudging Merric's shoulder.

Pausing at a fallen log, Merric finally dared a glance at me. "I rarely see anyone this far from the stables before midday. Most of the nobility who ride these paths aren't early risers, aside from you and your sisters." His lips twitched upward, as though tempted to smile but thinking better of it.

I barely contained a snort. "I'm impressed you managed to rise so early, yourself."

His brows rose in feigned confusion a second too late. "I beg your pardon?"

I stepped closer, lowering my voice to a hiss. "What do you think you're doing?"

"Well, Kirill here is supposed to be training to work with the guards, but he's been giving them some trouble. Lukas noticed he'd taken a liking to me and asked me to work with him. I was planning to see how he handles a variety of commands and determine whether there's anything in particular that sets him off."

My irritation bubbled over like a neglected stew. "You know that's not what I'm asking about."

He shrugged. "I'm sure you princesses don't train your own horses, so I could understand—"

I pinched the bridge of my nose. I *did* see him under that table, his face couldn't have been a figment of my imagination. "What were you doing at the ball last night?"

His jaw worked, his eyes studying the yellowed leaves creating an uneven rustling rhythm above us. As though coming to a decision, his gaze collided with mine. "I might ask you the same question." The frustrating man had the nerve to look defiant.

"Have you told anyone?" I winced at the panic leaking into my voice.

"The secret of your nighttime exploits is safe with me, Princess." The dry laugh that followed made it clear he spoke the title with little respect. "Though may I be so bold as to recommend you share at least a partial truth with your father? Of course you'd hate to be separated from your suitor, but the king deserves to know the dragons that plague him are there for your benefit."

"My *benefit*?" The word came out as a suppressed sob. "You think we *choose* to fly off at night to an enemy kingdom to be paraded around like prized hounds by those vipers?"

He opened his mouth, the fire in his eyes dwindling. "I...but you were all smiling and dancing. With the exception of one of your younger sisters."

"Poor Jolene." I sank down to where the fallen log formed a natural bench, too weary to continue standing. "We smile, we dance, we sit atop those terrifying creatures, we let Father suffer under the mystery of the dragons' tyranny, all for the same reason. Leonnar, the Crown Prince of Tsantar, never fails to remind us that if we don't play our part—if we tell our secret—he'll instruct his dragons to burn Kavalya Palace to the ground."

"Instruct..." Merric stretched a hand across his forehead to rub his temples. He looped Kirill's lead line around the nearest trunk and cinched it with a thick knot, then lowered onto the tree beside me. "Prince Leonnar is another Dragon Speaker."

Dragon Speaker? "I hardly know. But he does talk to the dragons. How else would he send them to Oneska whenever he has need of us?" My pulse slowed as I let his words catch up with my spinning thoughts. He hadn't told anyone. And he seemed to believe me, though why that mattered so much I couldn't fathom.

He pursed his lips. "People have found a variety of ways to interact and communicate with dragons. They're extremely intelligent. But only a Dragon Speaker has knowledge of *CxIyVhAuNz*. The dragon language." He tipped his head back, regarding a pair of squirrels chasing each other in an intricate pattern over and around swaying branches. "So this Prince Leonnar sends his dragons when he wants you to attend some social event, and you comply without telling anyone because he's threatening you."

"Yes. Which is why it's so critical you speak of this to no one." I glanced around, as though Leonnar or his brothers might materialize at the very mention of them. "If anyone in the Tsantarian royal family finds out someone knows the truth, they'll never believe us that we didn't tell. And if Father knew..." I suppressed a shudder. "We'd have a war on our hands."

"I understand." His brow creased. "But to what purpose? What good does it do them to force you to attend their balls and parties?"

"Leonnar claims the alliance his nobles and guests will assume we've formed adds to his popularity and power. But there's more..." My throat tightened around the words I hadn't even spoken to my sisters. "He recently explained there's some kind of sharing of the minds in a Tsantarian marriage ceremony, but only if both parties actually want to participate in the union." For some reason, that felt like the most important detail to include. "I imagine he knows he'll never get me to enter fully into a marriage like that, but he seems to think the odds might be better with one of my sisters." I hung my head. "I wish I could say with certainty that would never happen, but..." A shudder shook my shoulders. "If he were to acquire inside knowledge of all the workings of our kingdom—our guards, our industry, our allies—I have no doubt it would lead to disaster for Oneska. Or at the very least, an extremely one-sided partnership."

"No doubt." He nodded slowly, a storm brewing in his eyes. Sudden hope blossomed in my chest, as delicate as the petals adorning the surrounding shrubs. Someone knew our secret and seemed trustworthy enough to keep it.

What if he could help?

I sat bolt upright, startled by a new question now that we seemed to be safe from the dragons' wrath for the time being. "How did you get to Tsantar last night?"

He shifted. "I—followed you."

I frowned at his half-truth. "Obviously not on foot. Have you invented some flying contraption?"

"Now there's an idea." His mischievous smile was back, almost coaxing me to don a similar expression. It disappeared just as quickly as he rubbed his palms across his knees. "I rode a dragon as well."

I leaned forward, as though I could read his answer on his dirt-stained blue vest. "Were you riding with one of us? Without us noticing? Without the dragon noticing?"

"I'm afraid not." He shook his head. "That would've been an impressive feat indeed."

I waited for him to elaborate while he looked anywhere other than me. My tired sigh made me feel so much older than my twenty-one years. "You now know my darkest secret, Merric. One that could destroy this kingdom if you wanted it to. You owe me no confidences, of course, but if you know something that could help—"

"I do want to help, if I can, but I'm not sure..." He licked his lips. "I rode a dragon of my own to Tsantar. That is, not my own. Dragons should hardly be treated as pets or possessions. But a dragon friend of mine, I suppose you might say."

"A dragon *friend*?" I narrowed my eyes, waiting for humor or clarification to follow his statement. Surely no reasonable person could be friends with such creatures. At least no one who didn't have evil intentions like Prince Leonnar.

"Yes." The word stretched out to extra syllables. "I understand now why you would have a negative opinion of them, but no doubt the dragons used by Prince Leonnar are under as much duress as you and your sisters." Now he spoke quickly, as though racing to share thoughts held silent for too long. "Despite their size and power, dragons aren't vicious creatures at all. They're only violent when protecting their territory or young. Or subjected to the wrong person's control."

I nearly shrank back at his dark expression. But he seemed to know so much that might aid us. "Does a Dragon Speaker control dragons, then? Through their speech?" If my theory was correct... "Are *you* a Dragon Speaker?"

His gaze connected with mine, the entwined green and gold twisting my insides in an unsettling way.

"You are." The words drifted from me in an awed exhale. "Then you can help us!" I would've hugged the man if it wouldn't have been so inappropriate. The thought of resting in his strong arms sent a new twist to my stomach. *Focus, Emelia.* "If we find a way to sneak you up to the roof with us the next time the dragons appear, couldn't you just command them away? Instruct them to never return to Prince Leonnar?" My mind spun with possibilities. "Without the dragons to back up his threats, he'd be powerless to—"

He shook his head, cutting off my words. "I'm afraid it's not that simple."

My posture wilted. "You're not a Dragon Speaker?"

He glanced around, as though the correct answer were whispering on the breeze that ruffled our hair. "I am." He held out a hand like a parent fending off an over-excited child. "But it's an immense gift, to be granted knowledge of *CxIyVhAuNz*. I would hardly be a worthy Dragon Speaker if I were to go around commanding every dragon I encountered."

"Even when the dragons are being used for dishonorable purposes? Wouldn't you be saving them from an unworthy Dragon Speaker?"

He rose to his feet, tugging at the rim of his cap as he paced. "As I said, it isn't that simple. I can't just show up and force them to leave their master, as though they're slaves with no will of their own. It's possible they're choosing to serve Prince Leonnar, unlikely as that may be. Or directing them off might split up their families, leave them with no home to go to…"

I sat back, anger simmering beneath incredulity. "So you can help us, but you won't. The welfare of the dragons means more to you than that of your royal family. Of Callista, and Rosalind, and Jolene, and Pippa. And me."

I stood, refusing to let his pained look pierce my rage. He cared nothing for me, for my sisters, for our kingdom. Only for his revolting dragons. If my stomps back toward the path were more befitting of a toddler than a princess, so be it.

"Emelia. Your Highness. Wait, please. I'm not saying I refuse to help, only that—"

I kept my face angled away from him. "Thank you for your time. I've kept you from your work for too long." I took another step, then paused. "I trust you understand the importance of speaking to no one of this matter."

"Of course." His hesitance in the statement hinted he intended to say more.

I fled before he had an opportunity.

CHAPTER 9

I LAGGED BEHIND, ALLOWING the lively conversation of Calli, Duke Virkalt, and his cheerful sister—Hyacynthe?—to drift ahead. My boot caught on a stone, and I kicked it off the path with a clatter. Calli glanced back, her expression filled with concern and a bit of exasperation.

I'd been in a foul mood ever since my conversation with Merric the week before. Likely the reason she'd invited me to accompany her on this outing.

But it was a beautiful day, and I'd neglected poor Lyuda shamefully in my avoidance of the stables. Leaving me no reasonable excuse to refuse. Hopefully Merric was off on a trail, working with some nobleman, cleaning out a stall, or visiting his precious dragon friend.

The very idea made my blood boil. To think I'd considered him an ally, trusted him to help us escape the tyranny of Prince Leonnar and his dragons. Only to find out Merric controlled a dragon of his own. And seemed to admire the foul creature, beyond just appreciating the uses of its strength and fire.

I shivered and pulled my shawl closer around my shoulders. *It doesn't matter.* From what I could tell, Merric hadn't told anyone our secret, so we weren't any worse off than we'd been before.

Then why did my heart continue to ache every time I thought of the infuriating stable hand?

We reached the stable yard, and Calli spoke to Lukas about getting our horses saddled. Kirill stomped, kicking up a puff of dust from where he was tied to a fence post. Fortunately, with no rider in sight. I approached, letting him sniff my hand.

"Hi there, friend." I stroked his sleek neck, drawing calm from his warmth and earthy scent. "Are you heading out on a ride too? Or did you—"

"Princess Emelia."

My jaw tensed before the full significance of the familiar voice could register. "Merric." I dropped my hand and stepped back.

"I haven't seen you here in a while." He tugged at his leather vest, as though it had suddenly shrunk to a smaller size. "I...that is...I'm sure Lyuda misses you."

"As I miss her. I'm off to ride her right now, in fact." I forced my feet to take several more steps backward, refusing to be drawn in by his hopeful gaze.

"May I join you? Kirill could use some exercise, and if Lyuda gives you any trouble—"

"No." The word was too emphatic to be polite, but I hardly cared. I took a slow breath and gestured behind us. "I'm accompanying my sister Calli and her friends."

"Ah, of course." Was it my imagination that he looked disappointed? He closed the distance between us. "But, Princess Emelia, I really must speak with you at some point. I hope we can be friends again.

Or that we can at least clear up some misunderstandings from our last conversation."

I leaned closer, lowering my voice to a harsh whisper. "No friend of dragons is a friend of mine."

His hopeful expression crumpled, but he held my gaze. "I would appreciate an opportunity to change your mind."

I shook my head. "I have no interest in—"

"Please, Emelia. Princess." Red tinted his cheeks. "You would be in no danger. I truly want to help, and I'd like to be able to trust you with my...history with dragons."

Indecision tugged my heart and mind in two directions. Time with Merric did strange things to my insides, and I hesitated to let my guard down toward him again. But in my week away from the stables, I'd devised no new strategies to defeat the dragons on our own. Merric's help—questionable as it may be—was still our best lead by far.

"All right." I twisted my glove in my hands. "But I—"

"Emelia?" Calli's voice rang from the direction of the stable. "Oh, there you are." Her eyes lit with interest when she spotted Merric at my side.

Perfect. More speculation about Merric and myself is just what I need. "Coming." I turned back to Merric, brows raised.

He straightened his posture, returning his voice to a normal volume. "Shall we plan to work with Lyuda tomorrow, then?"

"Yes." I raised my chin. "I'll stop by in the morning."

"Thank you."

I broke away from the intensity of his gaze, feeling disoriented. My steps led me back to Calli and her duke without conscious thought. I mounted Lyuda, patted her neck, responded to polite inquiries from Duke Virkalt and Hyacynthe.

But my mind churned with the prospect of my meeting with Merric. Would he actually be willing to help us? Or would I fall under his spell once more, only to feel betrayed and disappointed yet again?

Back to the stables. I sighed, drawing in the crisp scent of falling leaves and fresh autumn air. Back to confusion, possibly frustration.

Possibly answers and hope.

My feet crunched faster down the path. If I was going to do this, I may as well get it over with.

The large, wooden structure of the stables came into view. Merric walked Kirill through some complicated exercises in the nearest paddock. I paused at the fence to watch. Whatever else he might be, the man certainly was an impressive horseman.

Lukas joined me. "Your Highness, good to see you. I hope you enjoyed your ride yesterday."

Tearing my gaze from Merric, I shifted to face him. "I did, thank you. Such lovely weather, and it was good to spend time with Lyuda."

"I can imagine. Shall I saddle her for you?"

"Oh, I..." I glanced to Merric, who had spotted us but seemed to be keeping his distance. "Yes, please. Thank you."

"Of course, Your Highness." Lukas also darted a look at Merric before bowing and heading toward the stables.

I gnawed on my lip. Finding an opportunity to talk with Merric might be more difficult than I anticipated, under Lukas's watchful eye.

Merric approached the fence, still on Kirill's back. "Good morning, Princess Emelia. I'm glad you decided to come."

I shaded my eyes, craning my neck to look up at him. "I hope I end up being glad I decided to come, too."

He huffed a laugh. "Kirill here always enjoys the paths, so perhaps we can…" His words trailed off as Lukas emerged from the stable with Lyuda.

It seemed the head stable hand could ready horses in record time.

"Here you are, Your Highness." He approached and handed me Lyuda's reins. "Do enjoy your ride."

"Thank you." I accepted his help to perch on the side saddle. "I'm planning to take that dirt trail up a way"—I pointed toward a gap in the trees—"if any of my sisters come looking for me."

Lukas smiled approvingly, and I caught Merric's subtle nod. With a wave, I nudged Lyuda into motion.

Hopefully Merric caught my meaning and would follow after Lukas became distracted with some other task.

No matter how many times I took this wooded trail, it always felt fresh and new. Different trees had blossomed into fall colors or turned into stark silhouettes after their leaves had shaken off. Familiar bird songs lifted in a new cadence, creating different harmonies and rhythms. I soaked it in, allowing Lyuda to travel the well-worn path with no instruction. Letting nature have its calming effect.

Prince Leonnar has no power over me here. Unless Tsantar decided to raze Oneska like they did to Philistra…

No. I clamped down on the devastating image, forcing my grip on Lyuda's reins to loosen. *We'll find another way.*

I brought Lyuda to a stop in the clearing where I'd attempted to teach Calli a few words of *CxIyVhAuNz.* Hopefully Merric would remember the spot. I looped Lyuda's reins around a tree and settled on the fallen log to wait.

Minutes later, hoof beats thundered up the path. Merric pulled Kirill to a quick halt when he spotted me. He leapt down with a small, sheepish smile. "I thought I'd better catch you before you changed your mind."

"Have you changed your mind?" I pressed my fingers into the rough bark, trying not to fidget.

Merric tied Kirill on the other side of the clearing before turning to face me. "There was nothing to change my mind about, Princess Emelia. I always intended to help."

My brows furrowed. "But—"

"I know." He raised his hands in a placating gesture. "But you have to understand. I realize it may be hard for you to trust me at this point, but I've had similar questions about your loyalties."

My protest came out in an embarrassing squawk.

Merric placed a hand on my shoulder as he lowered onto the log beside me. "Think back to that night in Tsantar when I followed you and your sisters. From my perspective. Based on what you'd hinted, you seemed distressed by the dragons' presence and wanted to be rid of them. Yet when I saw you at the ball, you were dancing and socializing. In *Tsantar* of all places." He spit the name of the kingdom like a curse. "It appeared you had hoodwinked your entire kingdom, including me, all for an opportunity to sneak away for clandestine flirtations with the enemy."

I shuddered at the unflattering image. "We would *never* willing-ly—"

"I know that now." He gave my shoulder a squeeze, then let his hand drop. "I believed your explanation, and it made much more sense based on my knowledge of Tsantar and what I've seen of you and your sisters." He stretched out his legs and crossed his boots at the ankles. "But within that one conversation, I went from thinking the worst of you to changing my mind to fielding a request to use my Dragon Speaking abilities on these unknown dragons. It was a lot to take in."

"That does make sense." I blew out a breath. The idea that he imagined for even a second that I wanted to be in Tsantar still stung, but it wasn't fair to fault him for the reasonable assumption. "But now that you've had some time to process, you'll use your abilities to free us from the dragons after all?"

He winced, and I turned to study some nearby goldenrod. Except I could hardly see it through the tears blurring my eyes.

He shifted beside me. "I want to help, Princess Emelia. More than anything."

I coughed to cover my sniffle.

"But not at the expense of those innocent dragons."

"Innocent?" I whirled on him. "When they've terrorized our kingdom for months, burned down the baker's home, forced my sisters and I to—"

"Not under their own volition." He pressed a handkerchief into my fingers. His warm hands squeezed my clenched fists before letting go. "Nothing they've done against Oneska has been their choice, of that I'm certain."

"Thank you." I dabbed at my eyes with the handkerchief. "But I don't understand how you can harbor so much loyalty toward such savage, violent beasts."

His shoulders drooped as he shook his head. "It's the violence of men like Prince Leonnar that causes them to be viewed in such a way. Just because they're powerful doesn't make them savage."

My lips twisted to one side. "You're trying to tell me those giants have a peaceful nature under that scaly, fire-breathing exterior?"

He relaxed against the nearest tree trunk. "Their fire and power were intended to protect and hunt for their families, not threaten and blackmail."

I shifted to face him fully. "They have families?"

He met my gaze with a warm smile. "Of course. You should see the way they guard their young. And how they let the littlest ones win in a race."

"You've seen such a thing?" I tried to imagine a light-hearted, caring scene play out among our dragon captors, but it didn't match with the hard glints in their vibrant eyes.

"I have." He brought his face closer, his eyes studying mine with an intensity that made it impossible to breathe. We were sitting too close, but I couldn't seem to back away. "I want to help you understand, Emelia, but it requires sharing some of the darkest moments of my past. Secrets that could take away my position here and condemn me to being an outcast once more, if the wrong person used them to twist my loyalties. Can I trust you with my story?"

"Yes." The word came out breathy as my mind fought to decipher his words amid the draw of my name spoken in his low baritone, his intense gaze and woodsy scent. I forced myself to blink and look down before I embarrassed myself further. "That is, I will keep your confidences as long as you pose no threat. Or unless certain pieces need to be shared with my sisters in order to gain our freedom."

"That is very reasonable. Thank you." He gave my hand a quick squeeze before settling back to a more respectful distance.

He tipped his head back, as though the crinkled leaves fluttering above held clues to how to proceed with his story. "I've been purposefully vague about my country of origin. Your sister, Princess Callista, seemed willing enough to brush it off as unimportant. But you, no doubt, noticed." The fond smirk he sent my way made my insides tighten all over again.

"Calli always believes the best of everyone." *I should've brought her along.* She managed to stay so much more even-tempered around this handsome, infuriating man.

He nodded, then intertwined his fingers in his lap. "I've been re-luctant to share because I hail from...Philistra."

CHAPTER 10

I JERKED FORWARD, MY eyes growing wide. "Philistra? But wasn't the entire kingdom turned into a wasteland? When it was ravaged by...dragons?" My thoughts spun into a tempest. Merric had survived the attack. Had others? His sympathetic view of the terrifying creatures was even more baffling knowing they had destroyed his homeland.

"That is correct." He shook his head, his expression filled with disgust. "Did you know that Prince Leonnar's father married a Philistran?"

"I—I had no idea."

"It seems they've tried to keep it quiet in recent years. Little wonder." His bitter chuckle was devoid of mirth. "But I remember my parents used to state it with such pride. Our little island had finally gained a powerful ally thanks to our brave princess." He winced at the horror that must've shone on my face. "Ironic, isn't it? Your explanation of the sharing of minds that takes place in a Tsantarian marriage confirmed my suspicions. While posing as our allies, Leonnar's father and grandfather must've mined her knowledge of Philistra's sources of wealth. Every one of our troves of gemstones and coral that made my country prosperous."

I squeezed my eyes shut. "That poor girl. I'm sure by the time she realized, it was too late." I couldn't let the same thing happen to one of my sisters.

He tilted his head. "It's hard to say when she might've realized. The events leading to our downfall started out seeming innocent enough. One of our mines was raided, but no one could find the culprit. Castle treasures were reported missing. Shipments of harvested coral mysteriously disappeared before reaching their intended destinations."

I pursed my lips as a thought struck me. "Did you live in the Philistran castle?" Maybe he wasn't a commoner at all, but had merely been reduced to these circumstances by the tragedy that befell his kingdom.

His jaw tightened. "I did."

"Then were you..."

"Royalty?" One corner of his mouth quirked, as though tempted to smile. "Thankfully, no. If I was, I'm certain the dragons' instructions would've prompted them to hunt and destroy me on sight. My father was a guard at the castle, and my mother found and tamed wild island horses. I joined her, once I was old enough." The warmth lighting his eyes faded. "When the dragons attacked, my mother sent me into a castle cellar."

"But she didn't stay with you?" I feared I already knew the answer.

He shook his head, his hair drooping against his forehead. "No. She must've known my father would be on the front lines defending the castle, and she wanted to find a way to help."

I scrunched the shimmering material of my skirt in confusion and anger. "But why would the Tsantarian king send dragons to attack if they were making off with your country's riches anyway?"

He shifted one leg onto the log, his fingers clenched tightly around one knee. "It only started that way—seemingly mysterious coincidences, so-called accidents that appeared to be a streak of bad luck. But my people weren't as naïve as the king hoped. As he grew in confidence, his men became sloppy, and Tsantar was implicated in a number of thefts. Angered and suddenly fearing for their future, the Philistrans began to revolt."

"Oh no." My mind shrank against the injustice of it all. People brave enough to rebel against the fate they must've known was inevitable.

He shrugged, brow furrowed as though his thoughts had followed the same path as mine. "They were small acts of rebellion at first. Refusals to follow the orders of the men King Pavel had put in charge, an uprising when a mine's shipment of night opal once again went missing. The Tsantarian king initially tried to stomp them out quietly, but the rebellions only grew and spread. I guess eventually he ran out of patience. Or perhaps ran out of riches to make little Philistra worth his trouble."

"I'm so sorry." Without pausing to think it through, I reached out and rested my hand on his.

"Thank you." With a wistful smile, he stretched his fingers to intertwine with mine. "I remember Father talking about it every night at dinner. He always had such a mixture of pride and fear in his voice as he detailed how our people were fighting the tyranny. Even his own contributions, in a few cases." He toyed with the pad of my thumb, sending a shiver to the tip of my spine. "No doubt he never realized how closely I was listening as I marched my toy soldiers across the floor."

"Your parents didn't survive the attack?"

"No." He traced the edge of my nail, then stiffened as though just realizing the familiarity of the gesture. "I'm not aware of anyone else from the castle who lived beyond that day." With a final squeeze, he dropped my hand.

A foreign mix of disappointment and relief tightened my throat. "But what happened to you?"

"I cowered in that cellar for hours. The sounds..." A shudder wracked his broad frame. "Then quiet. Almost worse than the screams, in a way. But even then, I stayed put. Lost in a strange trance half-panicked, half-asleep. When I couldn't take it anymore, I crept out and found...nothing. Piles of ashes in place of all the buildings, not a living creature in sight. The smell of smoke was almost unbearable. So I ran to a cluster of breadfruit trees that had survived. I felt less exposed and at least had something to eat. My sense of time was so hazy, but it was likely the next day that the dragons found me."

My hands tightened on the log. "Did they hurt you?"

"No." He shook his head emphatically, then regarded me with a sad smile. "They took care of me."

I blinked. Surely I'd misheard him. "Took care of you? But why—?"

"They had fulfilled the specifics of that monster's commands—there's no doubt in my mind that Leonnar's father is also a Dragon Speaker—so they had regained their free will. I was terrified when they first spotted me, of course, but they kept their distance. Even though we couldn't communicate, it wasn't hard to sense their regret. Sorrow, even. They seemed to hope that caring for the boy they'd orphaned would at least be a small act of atonement."

A tiny crack formed in the thick inner wall of ice I'd erected against the dragons. "But hadn't they been commanded to return to Tsantar? Did they take you with them?"

"There are limits on the compulsions. Relating to time, and I believe scope or perhaps the number of commands. I've never had any desire to test them." The earnest look was back in his eyes that appeared whenever he was defending his dragon friends. "But I'm certain King Pavel had no intention of relinquishing his dragons. He likely was on his way to retrieve them, but fortunately they regained their strength quickly enough to leave the area before he arrived. No doubt he hadn't wanted to risk being present for the actual fighting in case it endangered his royal head or produced witnesses of his treachery. Dragons are so feared and misunderstood, I imagine he had no trouble convincing people they'd attacked due to a slight provocation and completely without his knowledge or permission."

Thank goodness Prince Leonnar's elderly father chose not to attend most of the balls and parties in Tsantar. "So where did you go?"

He pressed his lips together. "If I'm honest, I don't know exactly. They helped me find food on what remained of the island. They seemed to surround me with a protective guard, though not close enough to make me alarmed. So when I could tell they wanted me to fly away with them, I couldn't think of a reason not to. There was nothing left for me—for anyone—in Philistra." His somber expression gave way to a grin. "I wish you could experience flying under more pleasant circumstances. When you have a choice and feel safe, it's the most amazing feeling. Especially when you're seven years old and have never left your island other than on a small rowboat."

The corners of my lips pulled upwards. "I can imagine how it would seem like a fun adventure to a young boy."

He rested the side of his head against his hand. "They flew to some remote mountainside in Therraci. Free from the interference and danger of any people, they built nests and cared for me as one of their own." His voice lowered to a reverent whisper. "I took it for granted at the time, but now I can appreciate what a unique experience it was."

Small wonder he was hesitant to speak about his past, especially when I'd shown such hatred toward dragons. "So they taught you their language in order to communicate with you?"

"No. Their language is so dangerous when entrusted to humans. Imagine teaching someone words they could use to control you."

I winced and nodded.

"For years, we used a laughable combination of gestures and sounds." He smiled, his gaze distant. "I suppose it developed into an unusual language of our own."

Years spent with dragons. Apparently, he wasn't exaggerating when he said he found animals easier to understand than people. "You learned it on your own, then? From being around them for so long?"

He shook his head. "*CxIyVhAuNz* can only be imparted by dragons. It's not taught piece by piece like by a schoolmaster, more like a magical transmission of the entire language at once."

"That's why only Prince Leonnar controls his dragons."

"Exactly." Merric sat up. "I'm sure the dragons in Tsantar are only allowed to give knowledge of *CxIyVhAuNz* when commanded so the dragons' power stays within the royal family." A hard glint darkened his golden eyes. "The exact opposite of how the language is meant to be used."

"Then what made them choose to teach you when you could already communicate with them?" I swatted away a fly, wanting to stay absorbed in his story.

He picked up a stray stick and began peeling the bark. "When I was ten, *FlAuVhIy*, the dragon I rode to Tsantar, had two hatchlings. They were too young to leave the nest, so she left me behind with them when the adults needed to hunt. Armed with my pocket knife and a homemade bow and arrow." He smirked and puffed his chest in a dramatic show of pride. "Not that there were many predators that high up in the mountains, especially with six dragons to be fed."

I stifled a giggle as his posture deflated.

"But storms stir up quickly in the mountains, and one day while I was alone with the hatchlings the wind blew so hard that the nest started tearing apart. I pulled down the tarp we'd hung to create my own shelter and secured it around the nest to keep out the wind and rain. *FlAuVhIy* was so grateful when she returned, she entrusted me with *CxIyVhAuNz*. It's a gift of great magnitude, but only to be used with respect and caution."

My gaze dropped to the fallen leaves clustered beneath my boots. "I apologize for trying to demand that you—"

"There's nothing to apologize for." He pressed my wrist. "Of course you only saw *CxIyVhAuNz* as a means to an end, the way Prince Leonnar does."

"Could you use your knowledge of *CxIyVhAuNz* to help in some other way?" My heart stuttered in an attempt to quench my anticipation.

"I believe so." His reply came out slow, cautious. "But not when they're here. I want to understand their full situation first to know how best to direct them. Do you know if there are additional dragons at Yrtulk Citadel?"

My breath caught. How had I not thought of that? "I don't know. But you're right, if we only freed some of them..."

"Prince Leonnar likely wouldn't take it well." He raised a brow.

"We need to wait and anger him when he has no dragons left to threaten us with."

"Precisely." He rubbed his palms together. "So I'll need to ride *FlAuVhIy* back to Tsantar and find out where they keep their dragons."

I bit my lip. "But that would be so much to take on by yourself. It's too dangerous."

"Only if I get caught." He shrugged. "Remember that I can control dragons, if necessary. I'll be fine."

I ran his plan through my mind again. It seemed so simple. Too simple, or just what we needed? "Where is *FlAuVbIy*? I find it hard to believe a dragon lives near Kavalya Palace without drawing attention."

"Not *that* near. She knows to keep her distance." He pursed his lips. "It's a fair ride up into the hills on the northern side of the palace. Kirill seems to enjoy the freedom of straying farther from the palace than normal."

I pictured the hills, shaking my head in wonder. A *dragon* lived among them. "But why is she here? I thought you said the dragons had settled in Therraci."

Merric tossed his now barren stick back to the ground. "When the dragons decided I was old enough that I needed to return to living with my own kind, *FlAuVbIy* wanted to keep an eye on me. Her own hatchlings are grown and settled with their own mates and families, though she does visit them from time to time. As I wandered, trying to find my place after years away from humans, I felt the most at home in Oneska."

"I'm glad." Our gazes met, a sudden dryness overtaking my throat.

"As am I." He leaned closer. "Thank you for hearing me out, Princess Emelia."

"Thank you for giving me another chance. I hope you don't come to regret trusting me or helping us." I blinked, forcing myself to break the unsettling connection. "Would you be willing to meet with my sisters? Before you go to Tsantar? I want them to understand our plan, and you'll be in a better position to explain. They should know that you're taking on such a risk for their freedom."

"If you wish." He took my hand. "But even if only your freedom hung in the balance, Princess Emelia, the risk would be well worth it."

CHAPTER 11

I paced the fireplace-adorned reading nook again, avoiding Calli's curious gaze. We'd checked the entire library twice to ensure we had the sprawling room to ourselves.

Still, worries plagued me.

What if Merric didn't come? What if my sisters objected to our plan? What if someone caught us meeting in here? What if—?

I shook my head, silencing the unhelpful thoughts. My sisters were just as affected by the dragon situation as I was. It was high time they got to know Merric better and understood how he planned to help.

If one of my sisters did think of a potential pitfall in our scheme, better to hear it now. And we'd stay alert. If someone else entered the library, there was nothing wrong with meeting Merric in a room of the palace that was open to anyone. That's why we'd chosen it. We'd act as though it was a casual encounter.

I wonder what Merric enjoys reading...

A knock sounded at the library door. One, then three in succession.

I turned, smoothing an imaginary wrinkle in my cascading blue skirt. "That's him."

Before I could step forward, Rosalind hurried to the door, Pippa at her heels. She opened the carved wooden door with a flourish, as though presenting royalty at a ball.

There stood Merric, clutching his hat in his hands, his expression a mix of stoicism and discomfort. He shuffled inside, giving a bow in our general direction.

"You must be Merric. Welcome." Rosalind presented her hand for a kiss, which Merric performed with awkward strain.

"Thank you."

She clicked her tongue. "My sisters failed to mention how handsome you are." The smile she bestowed upon Merric was glowing before she turned to me with an exaggerated pout.

Merric cleared his throat. "I suppose if beauty is in the eye of the beholder, their opinions may vary."

I couldn't interpret the wry look he sent my way. Did he think I didn't consider him handsome? Or was he teasing me? I didn't particularly like either alternative.

I squared my shoulders. "The subject likely wasn't raised because I hardly consider it relevant to the matter at hand."

"Speak for yourself." Rosalind shrugged and sent Merric a wink before crossing the room to lounge on the settee.

Pippa saved me from a response. "You're the one who let me canter on Natasa. I *knew* I saw you sneaking around at the ball!" She turned an excited glance my way before glaring at Rosalind. Returning her eyes to Merric, she tipped her head in thought. "I suppose I might consider you handsome, if you weren't so old."

Merric's delighted laugh brought a giggle to my own lips. At least the man didn't take himself too seriously.

"Too old for *you*, certainly." Calli patted Pippa's head as she steered Merric farther into the room. "It's a pleasure to see you again, Merric. Please, make yourself comfortable." She gestured to a velvet-lined armchair. "We so appreciate that you've come to guide and assist us."

The grateful smile he sent her in return made my stomach twist with an odd ache. I gave myself a mental shake. *Goodness, was I going to be jealous of all my sisters' interactions with this stable hand?*

"Yes, we are very thankful." My curt thanks felt like a shadow of Calli's exuberance, but the warmth in Merric's responding gaze made my thoughts slip away. I blinked and opened my mouth when Rose cut in.

"So what's the plan, then?" She raised a brow at me when I managed to turn her way.

I'd let them know that Merric planned to help and had knowledge that might allow us to escape the Tsantarian royal family once and for all. But I'd wanted Merric to be present for the full reveal so he could share only the details of his history he was comfortable with.

I perched on the edge of a wooden chair with a rounded gray cushion. "There's really nothing required of us, at all. Merric has experience with dragons, and it would only complicate matters if we were in Tsantar while he acts." I gestured to Merric but avoided his gaze.

"Right." Merric squirmed on his chair under the scrutiny of all five princesses. "If all goes well, Prince Leonnar will never be able to summon you again."

Jolene gave a contented sigh as she resumed clacking her crochet hooks.

"But how will you accomplish such a thing on your own?" Calli's tone radiated gentle concern.

His cheeks flushed. "It just so happens, I have my own means of traveling by dragon."

"I knew it!" Pippa bounced on her knees where she'd settled on the plush, golden-tasseled rug. "You followed us that night I saw you at the ball, didn't you? I knew I heard something behind me."

Merric smiled at her. "I thought I was being stealthy, but you're right. I followed all of you on my dragon, a little too closely it seems. I apologize if I frightened you."

Pippa gave a benevolent shrug. "Not after I saw your face under the table."

I'd found the sight anything but reassuring.

Merric chuckled. "So now my dragon friend knows where to find Yrtulk Citadel, and I don't need all of you to guide me. My hope is that you can stay safely at home while I free the dragons from Tsantar."

"Free the dragons?" Calli tilted her head in a bird-like movement. "Are you certain they want to be freed?"

Merric wrung the edge of his hat through his fingers. "I'll make sure of it before moving forward, but I can't imagine they wouldn't. It's not in the nature of dragons to threaten and terrorize innocent people. At least, when they're acting of their own accord."

"Prince Leonnar really is quite bossy." Pippa nodded with the imperious smirk of a gossiping matron.

I stifled a laugh as Rose leaned forward, raising a skeptical brow.

"But even if they want to be freed, how would you accomplish it?"

Merric glanced to me, and something passed between us. An almost tangible layer of trust, replacing the walls built from fear and apprehension. Then his attention shifted to Rose. "Thanks to my experiences with *FlAuVhIy*, the dragon I flew to Tsantar, I've learned to communicate well with dragons. She will take me to the citadel under cover of night. I'll sneak to where they house the dragons, undo any bonds that imprison them, and convince them that if they fly away they can be free."

"It sounds so simple." Calli regarded Merric with awe before turning to me. "You were right about focusing on the dragon language all along, Em."

I ducked my head. "It would've taken me years to do what Merric already can. If I ever managed to."

"But what about Flavy?" The name was almost unrecognizable under Calli's poor pronunciation. She gave a self-conscious giggle. "Your dragon friend. How will she stay safe while you seek out the Tsantarian dragons?"

"She'll merely take me to Tsantar, but far enough from the citadel that she won't be spotted. Then she'll return on her own. I'll ask one of the dragons under Prince Leonnar's charge to bring me back to Kavalya Palace before flying free."

"But if they're free..." Jo leaned forward, her voice timid. "Will they hurt anyone?"

"No." Merric shook his head. "If they're anything like the dragons I've known, they'll only want to live in peace. Far away from any sign of civilization. They need to hunt for food, but they'd never hurt a person unless provoked."

Calli grasped Merric's arm. "What a brave, beautiful thing you're doing for those dragons. And for us."

I nodded, but it felt so inconsequential. Why couldn't I phrase things—affect people—the way Calli could?

Merric glanced at Calli, then around to the rest of us. "I'm simply grateful that I happen to possess the knowledge to right this wrong. Prince Leonnar has taken advantage of those dragons and you princesses for far too long. He needs to be stopped."

"And now we have our hero ready to take action." Rose fluttered her eyelashes at Merric with a coy smile.

"But we should let Merric prepare himself, since he plans to act tonight if Leonnar doesn't send for us." My voice came out more clipped than I intended, but I needed to get Merric out of here before he became enamored with both Calli and Rose.

I wouldn't stop to ponder why that prospect bothered me so much.

Merric stood, directing a grateful smile my way. "Yes, I should gather what I need to bring and think through my strategy once more. With any luck, you should never need to see Prince Leonnar again."

Calli and Rose of course beamed at him, and Jolene glowed with a quiet hope. Only Pippa bit her lip, bearing no trace of her earlier enthusiasm.

Maker, send her someone new who will be more deserving of her affections. And help her to be content in the meantime.

I turned to Merric, who hovered uncertainly. He bowed. "Well, then, I—"

"Shall I accompany you?" The words came out before I could add any poise or subtlety.

Behind Merric, Rose rolled her eyes with a smirk. *Lovely.* I must appear as flirtatious as she was.

Except far less successful.

Heat searing my neck, I stumbled to think of a way to retreat.

But Merric stepped closer, offering his arm. "I would appreciate that, Princess Emelia. Thank you. No doubt I'll come up with additional questions about Yrtulk Citadel as we walk."

I placed my hand on his arm, taking in his steadiness and warmth. He began at a leisurely pace out of the library, and I followed suit, trying to ignore the tension in my legs that wanted to flee the curious, amused gazes of my sisters.

"It's a joy watching you with your family." Merric patted my hand that rested on his arm.

I laughed. "Thank you for braving so many of us at once. I'm sure we're a lot to take in for anyone who isn't accustomed to our chatter."

He shook his head. "Not at all, it's exactly how siblings should be. Comfortable with each other, supportive but with some good-natured goading." His shoulders drooped as he sighed. "I often wished for siblings as a child."

I squeezed his arm. "I'm sorry you were denied that experience. Though wonderful as they are, my sisters and I cause plenty of trouble for each other."

"Oh, I can tell." He didn't bother to hide his chuckle. "That Pippa doesn't hold her tongue."

"Never in front of us, though she behaves tolerably in public." I braced myself, waiting to see what he would have to say about Calli. Or Rose.

But he pulled me the slightest bit closer. "It's clear how much they all look up to you."

I shrugged. "Ever since we lost Mother..."

He patted my hand again, this time letting his linger. Though such a small contact, the warmth traveled up my arm to my core.

I attempted a shrug. "Well, they probably view me more as a mother than a sister. The younger ones, at least." Unbidden tears pricked at my eyes. "I've felt so helpless these past months, seeing them subjected to Prince Leonnar's whims and threats. We're so grateful that you—"

"I know." His gaze held mine. When had we stopped walking? "I'm only sorry it's taken me so long to act."

I swallowed against the lump growing in my throat. "It took me a while to allow you to help."

His smile drew my attention to his mouth. I averted my gaze, my stomach in all kinds of knots. Anxiety for Merric, of course, but also something more...pleasant.

Summoning what little sanity I had left, I turned to keep walking. Merric complied, but were we walking even closer than before? I glanced around the corridor, but it was empty aside from a guard at the far end.

Merric gave my hand a final pat, then released it. "Now that we're working together, Prince Leonnar doesn't stand a chance against us."

Please, Maker, let him be right.

I wandered back to the stable yard, worry clenching my insides as though I were wearing Pippa's stays. I kicked up a cloud of dirt as the smells of hay and horse manure grew stronger.

Where is Merric? Why hasn't he contacted us?

I ached to see him, to know whether he'd been able to set the dragons free as planned. But already the sun dipped toward the horizon, soon to bathe the sky in rays of pink and orange. A full day had passed since I'd bid Merric farewell, the hopes and safety of me and my sisters on his shoulders. Had something prevented him from going to Tsantar? But surely he would've let us know. Perhaps after the long night he'd slept the day away? Or he'd remained with *FlAuVhIy?*

I'd yet to determine a way to search for or inquire about his quarters that wouldn't cause embarrassment and scandal.

The erratic beat of my heart told me something had gone wrong, but I fought to ignore it. Surely there were plenty of alternative explanations...

"Your Highness." Lukas hailed me with a shallow bow. "Weren't you here earlier today?" He brushed at the stray oats clinging to his vest.

Twice, but I didn't plan to mention that to him. "Yes." I snatched at the first explanation I could conjure. "Merric was going to try a new calming technique for Lyuda when she gets restless. I was curious if he had any success, but I couldn't find him the first time I stopped by. Have you seen him?"

"I've yet to see any of this trouble you've said Lyuda's been causing." He rubbed his knuckles against his jaw.

"It's only on occasion, and of course you keep so busy." I clamped my mouth shut. My words were bubbling out too fast for any appearance of calm.

"I suppose I do." He stretched out the words, clearly not convinced. "But no, Merric requested the day off. He's a hard worker, so I figured he'd earned a bit of fun." He narrowed his eyes. "I'm surprised he didn't tell you, with all the personal attention he's given your horse."

I shrugged, feigning nonchalance. "Perhaps he did, I don't recall. No matter, I was planning to go for a ride with my sisters tomorrow anyway. Thanks for your help."

Rather than return to the horse he'd been leading toward the paddock, he kept his gaze on me. "I don't want to speak out of turn, Your Highness, but don't encourage Merric so much that he forgets his place. I've seen the way he admires you. Not that I can blame him, but of course a stable hand wouldn't be fit for our Crown Princess."

Warmth and irritation swirled in a dizzying haze. Did Merric admire me? I shook off the thought. Much as I wanted to disagree, Lukas was right. And what mattered far more right now was that Merric was missing. "I appreciate your concern, but Merric has been nothing but professional and respectful. Good day."

Once I'd gained some distance from the stables, I let my carefully trained expression fall. *Now what?* I'd need to dress for dinner soon, and I'd made no progress finding out about Merric's mission.

A shadow passed, and I glanced up. Far overhead, a dragon soared above the points of the tallest pines. Then another. Indigo scales, followed by golden, emerald, peach, and scarlet. They drifted toward the right until they came to a landing on the rooftops of Kavalya Palace.

No. Heat and cold cycled through my limbs like a fever, making me tremble. They were back, they hadn't been freed.

So where was Merric?

CHAPTER 12

"We had an interesting visitor last night." Prince Leonnar's posture was casual, but his words were oddly strained.

My jaw tensed, my thoughts straying to Merric as they'd done all evening. *Stay neutral, Em. Leonnar could be talking about anyone.* "You seem to have many interesting visitors coming and going at any given time."

"True. But they're usually invited." His gaze hardened as he swung me in a tight circle.

"Those are certainly the ideal visitors, yes." I pursed my lips as I tapped my foot in rhythm with the drums. "I suppose someone wanted an opportunity to view the luxury and grandeur of Yrtulk Citadel? Or an old acquaintance planning a surprise?"

"Hmm. Perhaps *you* can tell *me*." He tightened his hold on my waist, stroking the fingers of his free hand along his closely-cropped facial hair. "I'd never seen the man in my life, and he hardly seemed drawn by the luxury. In fact, he wasn't anywhere near the guest quarters of the citadel. He was found sneaking around our dragon enclosure."

My stomach sank at the same time my heart leapt into my throat. But I could process the implications later. For now I had to keep dancing, keep talking as though terror for Merric's safety didn't consume me. "Interesting, indeed. They are impressive creatures, perhaps he wanted a closer look. Or do you suspect he meant to steal them?"

His chuckle seemed to exhibit genuine amusement. "They could not be stolen." His tone conveyed a warning. "Whatever his purpose, it landed him in the prison." He flicked his hand, as though dismissing a beetle.

No. I forced my expression, my posture, my breath to give no sign of my inner turmoil. *Protect him, Maker.*

"I almost thought to ask if he had any connection to you and your sisters. Since your fellow countrymen have exhibited such distaste for my dragons in recent weeks." His intense gaze watched my every move, until I felt more like a caged animal than a dancer at a ball.

I puckered my nose. "You thought we sent a strange man to visit your dragons? For what reason? Did he try to hurt them?" The concern on my face was very real, but not for the dragons. "Besides, it would take days for someone to get here from Kavalya Palace without an *escort*."

The music ended, but he kept a tight grip on my arm. "There was no indication he intended to hurt the dragons. He carried no weapons aside from a paltry knife. My guards couldn't ascertain how he arrived, a lapse that will be dealt with." He let go but kept his eyes fixed on me. "I couldn't help but wonder, you must understand."

"Hasn't the man given some explanation for his actions?" My stomach squirmed. Much as I didn't want Merric to reveal anything about our plan, I also hated the thought of our secrets causing him further trouble.

He shrugged. "I haven't asked him yet. We find our prisoners are more willing to talk if they have some time to think things through."

My mouth dropped open. "Do you at least give them food and water? What if you subject someone to the darkness and stench of the dungeon, only to find upon questioning that they were innocent?"

He chuckled, leading me to a table of refreshments. "Few people are truly innocent, my naive Emelia." He handed me a glass of fizzing champagne. "But our prison isn't as terrible as all that. You may be less eager for an alliance between our kingdoms than I, but that doesn't make me a monster. Not only do we feed and water our prisoners, but they even have access to fresh air."

I swirled the liquid in my glass, the strange churning of guilt and hope in my chest making the saccharine drink even less appealing than usual. "You don't keep your dungeons underground, then?"

"There's no need." He drained the remainder of his champagne and hailed a servant to fetch his glass.

My mind raced through everything I'd seen of Yrtulk Citadel. Would a rescue be possible? If there were multiple points of access, perhaps...

"Emelia." He lifted my chin, forcing me to look at him. "I'm no monster, but I'm also no fool. Use of an island off our coast made it easy to create cells that are both isolated and quite challenging to access. Unless you know your way through the underground tunnels."

I tossed my head with what I hoped was a flippant air. "Of course *I* would never seek to access them." I gave an exaggerated shudder. "But I am glad to hear you don't starve your prisoners, leave them in complete darkness, or some other form of cruelty. Oneska certainly has no interest in allies who would allow such inhumane conditions."

"Indeed." He raised his brows in a silent challenge, then motioned back to the center of the room for the next dance.

I'm a fool. But whether because I was seeking out a dragon or because I had no idea where to find that dragon was anyone's guess.

Likely both.

Regardless of my mounting fears and the sensible thoughts trying to poke holes in my faulty plan, I let Kirill take me onward. He navigated the thin, dusty path with practiced ease, his ears flicking at an occasional bird's call or persistent ladybug.

Merric had to be the prisoner Prince Leonnar had described the night before. The thought of him languishing in the prison, even with food and water, had tortured me all night. He'd been caught trying to help *us*. I had to at least try to see him, to set him free if possible. But the only way to get to Tsantar with any speed was on the back of a dragon.

My flimsy hopes of finding *FlAuVhIy* rested on Kirill remembering the way. The stable hand who'd saddled him for me seemed taken aback, but at least he hadn't questioned me the way Lukas would've.

But what if Kirill hadn't taken this path often enough to send us in the right direction? What if I'd misunderstood Merric's description of where *FlAuVhIy* lived in these hills?

I took a calming breath, letting it settle the questions that raced as quickly as my pulse. *Then I'll just enjoy this lovely day and come up with a different plan tomorrow.* Merric's absence nagged at my conscience and heart, but this nearness to his favorite horse, heading to a spot he presumably felt drawn to, brought an odd sort of comfort.

Kirill veered off the worn path, and I gripped the reins to keep my seat. *What—?* Ahead, traces of broken branches and nibbled grass indicated this wasn't his first time taking this unexpected route.

I patted his neck. "Carry on, Kirill. I trust you." *I trust you too, Merric. At least I'm trying to.*

We crossed the valley between two hills, still surrounded by trees and following a path I couldn't discern. A bit unsettling, but hopefully a good sign. Kirill surged ahead, tugging at the reins.

"Easy, boy. I'm not sure..."

He ignored me and kept tugging forward. We broke through the tree line, and he gave a satisfied snort before breaking into a trot.

I relaxed into the faster gait with a quiet laugh. "You knew this was coming, didn't you?"

He sniffed and smoothed his strides into a canter. I closed my eyes, smiling into the wind that blew hair from my face and caressed my cheeks. *We'll get you back here, Merric. You deserve to enjoy this, too.*

At the far end of the meadow, Kirill slowed. He sniffed around the trees until he seemed to find the one he was looking for.

I braced to enter another bramble of rustling leaves and tugging branches, but he lowered his head to graze. Shading my eyes, I scanned the area more carefully. Had we reached our destination? Whatever destination that might be.

But there was no more sign of a dragon here than at Kavalya Palace. I massaged my forehead.

Apparently, this had been a fool's errand, indeed.

Then I glanced back down at Kirill, who continued to munch grass at his leisure. Merric could hardly take a horse right up to a dragon's lair and expect him to be willing to return.

"Merric leaves you here, doesn't he?"

Kirill didn't grace me with a reply.

I slid off his back and found a spot on a nearby trunk to tie his lead line. Hopefully, he wouldn't feel any need to test my fumbling knot. I stretched my legs and gave the clearing another perusal. Now what? Kirill may have brought me significantly closer to Merric's dragon, but without him to lead me the rest of the way...

I paced the tree line, searching for places Merric might've tramped through the underbrush. With a sigh, I turned back toward Kirill. He'd wandered far enough that his lead line stretched almost taut. He kept his head down, drinking from a tiny trickle of a stream. My breath caught. Dragons needed water too, right? Could it be that simple?

With a pat to Kirill's back as I scurried past, I followed the depression of the stream up into the forest. *Please, lead me to Merric's dragon.*

And let her not be too terrifying.

My skirts snagged on another branch. I pulled them free with a huff. *Merric, just how far from the dragon do you leave your horse?*

Unless I was on the wrong route entirely...

No, I hadn't covered enough distance to give up hope yet. Merric would've traveled faster, after all, with knowledge of the path and no dress to hinder him.

Just as the thin line of water took me to the crest of a hill, it dipped down again. How could one little rivulet be so meandering? Presumably it flowed more heavily during the spring and summer months.

I hiked up my skirts and picked my way down the steep face of the hill. I glanced toward the sun, which was making a similar descent. A bit farther, but then I'd have to give up if I wanted to be home before...

An opening in the trees allowed for a much broader view, and I gasped. On the far side of the valley, the terrain turned rocky. Tan and red-marbled stone stretched flat before climbing the next hill over, creating a cave-like enclosure.

The surrounding grass looked trampled and a bit singed.

Ignoring the fear bubbling in my midsection like fizzing champagne, I increased my pace. I tore down the remainder of the hill and stumbled onto the smooth stone, nearly tripping at the change in texture.

My gaze scanned the area in half excitement, half trepidation. But despite signs of a dragon's presence, the actual dragon was nowhere to be seen. *No, no, no. I can't fail after all this.* Did she and Merric arrange to meet at a certain hour somehow, and the rest of the time she lived elsewhere? Was she out hunting?

I shuddered, sending up a quick prayer for Kirill back at the clearing.

"Hello? Is anyone here?" No birds chirped in reply, no squirrels rustled through the leaves. Almost eerily quiet. Could that be the sign of a dragon after all? "*FlAuVhIy?*" The strange syllables felt malformed in my mouth. "Are you here somewhere? I—"

A familiar snort sounded from the direction of the rock face, and I stifled a scream. A dragon with black scales that glittered like onyx stepped from the crevice, scanning until her gaze landed on me. Though every bit as massive and intimidating as the dragons in Tsantar, her eyes seemed less hostile. Softer, though a bit wary.

"Um, hello. Greetings." I lowered into a curtsy. "Thank you for coming out to meet me. I am Princess Emelia of Oneska."

She leaned closer, eyes narrowed in confusion. *Right. She doesn't understand me.*

"I'm sorry, I'm not a Dragon Speaker." I shook my head. "I don't know *CxIyVhAuNz*."

She lowered her head, studying me. My pulse galloped, making my temples throb, but I stood my ground.

"I come as a friend of Merric."

Her neck swiveled, as though hoping to find him with me.

"He's not here. Merric is in trouble." Saying the words aloud gripped my chest in an iron fist.

She glanced back at me.

"Merric was captured." I mimed clamping manacles around my wrists. "In Tsantar." I pointed to the south, as if she could somehow see fifty miles in that direction.

At the word Tsantar, she tensed. *Maybe some of this is getting through to her, after all.*

"Merric needs our help to set him free." I demonstrated unclasping the pretend bands around my wrists.

Her expression seemed...concerned? Or maybe just confused.

"Could I return and ride on your back?" I pantomimed climbing up her scales, then extended my arms like I was flying. "To Tsantar to save Merric?"

"Tsantar." The word sounded familiar, yet oddly foreign in her gravelly voice. "*IyJp* Merric."

"So you'll help?"

She dipped her head in what I hoped was a nod.

Hope burst in my chest like rays of sunlight. Despite my terrible attempt at charades, I was communicating with a dragon. Guilt tweaked my conscience at the ways I'd railed against the creatures in the past. Perhaps Merric was right, and they weren't so bad after all.

Perhaps.

FlAuVbIy shifted to face southward and then crouched, giving me an expectant look.

She was ready to head to Tsantar right now? The hard layer of hatred I'd built up against dragons softened a bit more. She must truly care about Merric. No wonder he considered her a friend.

But desperate as I was to check on Merric, I couldn't just disappear for the rest of the evening. And if this attempt at reaching Merric went awry...

I shook my head. "Thank you, but not yet. Tomorrow, or the next day." I pointed as though counting days, not that a dragon would likely have any concept of a calendar. "At night." I motioned toward the sun, lowering my hand to mimic sunset, then pretended to sleep.

She gave a smaller nod. "*VhOeBr.*"

"I will come back." I walked my fingers away before turning them back toward her.

Her lips curved as a soft exhale huffed through her nostrils. Was she laughing? Apparently, there was a great deal I didn't yet understand about dragons. She flapped a wing and turned toward her cave.

"Goodbye for now. Thank you."

I tripped back down the path toward Kirill, my heart lighter than it had been in weeks. In a day or two, I would get to see Merric.

And I had a dragon for an ally.

CHAPTER 13

"You did *what*?" Calli's usually serene composure splintered like a dropped glass.

"Shh." I searched the remote corner of the garden where we'd perched on a bench, but only a pair of jays seemed disturbed by my sister's outburst. "I found Merric's dragon friend. I'm going back there tonight, assuming we aren't summoned by Prince Leonnar."

"And then you're planning to ride her to Tsantar?" Calli's brows arched high.

"Yes, I have to check on Merric. To save him if I can." I paused to inhale, but the heady floral scent barely registered in my anxious state. "Not knowing what they've done to him—"

"I know." Calli gripped my hand, her gaze softening. "I'm worried too, and I've seen how the two of you... Anyway, I would also appreciate reassurance that he's well."

I ducked my chin, feeling a rush of warmth despite the autumn breeze. What exactly did she suspect was going on between myself and

Merric? And did her suspicions have any grounding in reality? I shook my head.

Those questions could only become relevant once Merric was no longer a prisoner of Tsantar.

"But it's so dangerous, Em." She gnawed her lip, a line creasing her forehead. "Even if Merric trusts this dragon, we have no guarantee she won't harm you. And what if you get caught?" She shuddered.

Across the path, hydrangea clusters had faded from vibrant pink to brittle tan. I felt an odd kinship with them as Calli's questions brought my own fears rushing back. "Those concerns have plagued me as well. Believe me, if there were any other way, I'd take it. But Leonnar would never willingly set him free, especially if he finds out Merric's connection to us and knowledge of dragons. Unless maybe I agreed to marry him."

"Never." Calli tightened her grasp. "You're right, I suppose. It must be done." She straightened. "And I'm coming with you."

"What? No." It was my turn to disturb the garden's animal inhabitants. I lowered my voice to a harsh whisper. "It wouldn't do for both of us to be in danger."

"But what if something goes wrong? What if you need help, and—"

"Calli." I took her other hand in mine. "I appreciate the offer, and I can't deny that your presence would bring some comfort. But it will be even more comforting to know that you're home safe. That someone other than Leonnar knows where I am." I squeezed her fingers, willing her to understand. "That someone will be here to care for Pippa and Jo, and even Rose, if I'm not able to return."

"Oh, Em, you always take too much upon yourself." A sheen glistened in her earnest gaze. "But if you insist, I will let you go alone. I'll be praying all night."

"Thank you, I'll need that." Now tears blurred my own vision.

Calli released my hands and wrapped me in a hug. "Go find your Merric."

I coughed. "He's hardly *my*—"

She pulled back far enough to give me a fond smile. "He would be, with the merest word or look from you."

The thought sent a flutter through my chest, but surely her optimism and sisterly affection had fueled her imagination.

"But be careful. Come back to us." She tightened her arms around me, and I drew strength from her embrace.

I'd find a way to free my sisters, somehow. But first, I had to find Merric.

FlAuVbIy soared high over Yrtulk Citadel. Hopefully too high to be noticed. Beyond, the ocean lapped in gentle waves that reflected torchlight from the shore.

I could come to appreciate this place, if not for the people who live here.

The dragon's wings flapped faster as the island came into view. No doubt her thoughts mirrored mine. *Merric is trapped somewhere on that barren piece of rock.*

As we'd planned in our awkward attempts at communication, she continued to fly high above the ocean for a distance past the island before circling back. She descended to hover just above the water, using the prison to hide us from view of the citadel.

With nearly silent footfalls, she landed on the wide, flat slab of rock. In this dim lighting, the prison almost appeared to rise as part of the rock formation, except for its perfectly circular shape. At evenly-spaced intervals, rectangular slabs were removed from the structure at face level, filled in with vertical metal bars.

My heart sank as I took in the solid rock of the structure, the small size of the windows. Even with a dragon's help, I'd never rescue Merric from out here. The poor man would have to stay in his prison cell a while longer.

But which one?

I slid down from *FlAuVhIy's* back, clutching the bundle of food I'd wrapped in a blanket. *At least I have some small comfort to offer him in the meantime.*

Voice low, I turned to *FlAuVhIy*. "How do we find him?"

She angled her head closer, but of course she couldn't understand me.

"Merric. Where?" I pretended to search for something.

She perked up, nostrils flaring. She gave a soft snort, then walked in a wide arc toward the next cell window, if it could be called that.

Could she *smell* him?

She continued assessing each small window from a distance, dismissing several more. Loud snores emanated from one cell, but whatever other inhabitants might be within remained quiet.

Two windows past the snoring prisoner, *FlAuVhIy* stopped with a huff and tipped her head toward the building.

"This one? That's Merric?"

Her large head bobbed in a nod.

"All right. Then you should be off for now, but I'll whistle when I'm ready." I mimed her flying away and myself whistling, then gave her neck a tentative pat. "Be careful."

She nudged my hand with another nod. Her gaze seemed wistful as she looked toward what she'd claimed was Merric's cell. *She cares for him too, in her way.* With a snuffle that puffed my hair, she took off and soared over the moonlit ocean.

I was on my own now, but *FlAuVhIy* had gotten me this far. I had to trust her assessment of which cell was Merric's, trust that she'd come back when I whistled... *Trusting a dragon.* I shook my head.

I guess even dragons are more trustworthy than Prince Leonnar.

Muscles tense, I crept toward the nearest window. Even my breathing felt too loud on this quiet island. With a rueful smile, I sent up a prayer of thanks for the snoring that at least provided a hint of background noise.

Reaching the window, I tried to peer in. The cell seemed to narrow to a thick door on the far side, but I couldn't make out any further details in the dark. *Please let FlAuVhIy be right.* "Merric?" I paused, holding my breath. The snorer rumbled on, and no other prisoners made a sound.

At least this cell was on the far side of the island, out of view of the citadel.

I leaned even closer and tried again. As I strained my eyes to see if anyone was inside, a figure shifted with a moan. Guilt and sympathy tugged at my heart, tightening my chest.

"Merric? Is that you?" No matter how hard I squinted, I couldn't get a better look to verify his identity.

The man sat up and rubbed his forehead. "What—?" His eyes widened almost comically as he turned toward me.

Definitely Merric. A surge of relief mixed with something I didn't have time to dwell on filled me at the sight of his face. He was alive, capable of speech and movement. Still a captive, but the tension in my shoulders relaxed as the worst of my fears slipped away.

"Pri...Em?" He shook his head as though trying to remind himself where he was. "But how?"

"Yes, I'm here." Warmth flooded through me at his use of my nickname. It sounded right, somehow. A sign of affection rather than disrespect.

Stop it, Emelia. It has everything to do with caution and nothing to do with how he might feel about you.

I tightened my jaw, dismissing the distracting thoughts. "Are you all right? What have they done to you?"

"Nothing that won't heal." How the aggravating man loved his vague responses. "But how are you here? Did they capture you too?" Panic quickened his speech as he hurried to the window to peer out through the bars.

"No, they haven't caught me. At least not yet." The phrase sounded more flippant than I felt.

"It really is you." His eyes widened with wonder once more. "I thought I must be dreaming." He slid his fingers through the bars, as though seeking to ascertain I was a physical being instead of a ghost.

Inching closer, I squeezed his fingers in one of my hands. As cold as I'd feared, with this open window and no fire to warm the space. "Surely you could conjure a more pleasant dream than a visit from a grumpy princess. But yes, it's me. And I brought something for you." I took out the dried fruit and meat and rolls piece by piece and handed it between the bars, then scrunched the blanket until he could slide it through.

"You are an angel." He shook out the blanket and wrapped it around himself, then returned his fingers to my hand that rested on the window ledge.

Heat colored my cheeks at the thought that he relished the small touch as much as I did. "Hardly. But at least it's a little something." Hopefully the dark hid my flaming face.

"Thank you, Em. Truly." His fingers caressed my palm, sending a pleasant tingle up my arm.

"How terribly are you hurt? Do you have water and food and—"

His smile shone in the moonlight. "Warmer and about to be better fed thanks to you. The guards only roughed me up a bit. I've certainly had plenty of time to nurse my injuries." A hint of frustration marred his attempt at a cheerful tone.

"I so wish I could free you tonight, but we're not ready yet." I shifted against the cold seeping through my dark gray dress.

He shook his head, displacing a wave of tawny hair across his forehead. "No, don't worry about me. Much as I hate to send you away, you mustn't be here. Please." He brought his face close to the bars, his eyes pleading as much as his whisper.

"I can't leave yet. I wanted to see how you're faring and give you a few tiny comforts, but I had another reason for coming as well." I leaned closer too, as though it would make a difference in whether we were overheard. "We're coming up with a new version of the plan. One that includes rescuing you."

"You are incredible, Emelia. You and all your sisters. But focus on freeing yourselves, don't return to this awful prison." He frowned. "You never did tell me how you got here."

"Ah, well." I swallowed. Would he be upset that I sought out *FlAu-VhIy*? But he was stuck in prison because he'd tried to help us. He deserved the truth. "I recruited some help from your friend."

"My friend?" He tilted his head in confusion. "Someone from the stables?"

"No." I brushed off some of the dirt that had accumulated on my skirt. "A friend who can fly."

"*FlAuVhIy?*" He breathed her name with incredulity, but not anger.

"Kirill and I rode up into the hills like you described. I didn't know how else to get here unseen." I forcibly hushed my tone, wanting to keep explaining at the top of my lungs if it would erase that pucker from his brow and help him to believe my good intentions.

He blinked slowly, lines still creasing his forehead. "You found *FlAuVhIy* and got her to fly you here? But how did you communicate? And where is she?"

"Yes. She at least recognized your name, and once she knew you were in trouble she was eager to help. I never was much good at charades, but we managed." I shrugged with a self-conscious laugh. "She let me off on the island and sniffed you out, I think? Now she flew off to somewhere she'll be safe until I call her back."

Merric's fingers tensed. "Emelia..."

"I'm sorry. I didn't mean to put your friend in danger, but I didn't know what else to do. I—"

"Em." The soft, almost tender whisper cut through my panic.

I leaned toward him, drawn by the warmth of his intent gaze.

His fingers reached through just enough to brush my cheek. "I'm not angry. I couldn't be more impressed. I know how you feel about dragons, how you've been forced to interact with them under the worst of circumstances. Yet you overcame that fear for a lowly stable hand whose trustworthiness you question."

"I do trust you." He couldn't know how much that statement cost me, but the truth of it sank into my very soul. I'd somehow gone from feeling anger and suspicion toward this foreigner to something very different. "And you're no mere lowly stable hand. You were caught trying to help us."

"Please, don't feel any guilt on my account. I'd do it again without hesitation. I just wish I'd succeeded." He lowered his hand with a grimace. "I only needed another minute or two. But Prince Leonnar got there too fast. The dragons were still within hearing range, and he managed to call them back."

I winced. *To be so close...* "How many were there?"

"Eight. All held in the same enclosure on the back side of the citadel. Heavily guarded." His voice lacked its usual confidence and buoyancy.

"Don't give up, Merric. Keep yourself alive and as healthy as you can until we get you out. Our plan may yet succeed." I tried to pour every ounce of optimism I wanted to feel into the statement. "But I need your help. We need a Dragon Speaker if we're ever to set the Tsantarian dragons free. Can you...can you teach me?"

He shook his head, his expression shifting from frustration to sadness.

"I wouldn't use it against them, Merric. You have my word."

His smile was sweet but tinged with regret. "I know you wouldn't. But such a task is beyond the skills of a mere man. Only a dragon can transfer knowledge of *CxIyVhAuNz*, remember?"

"That's right." Such a key detail to forget. I sank against the cold stone with a sigh, mind spinning.

Resolve settled in my chest, heavy but firm. We couldn't give up that easily. "But I only need a few key phrases to set them free, if used at the right moment. Could you teach me that much?"

His mouth twisted to the side as he ran a hand over his hair. "You do have an unusually good ear for *CxIyVhAuNz*." He set his jaw, his lips pressed into a thin smile. "Let's give it a try."

CHAPTER 14

"Did you see Merric? Did you bring him back?"

"You *chose* to ride a dragon?"

"You were gone *all night*?"

My sisters' questions blew about our chamber like a tempest as I closed the door behind me and hung up my cloak. I rubbed my tired eyes. I'd returned Kirill to a surprised Lukas, claiming a desire for an early morning ride and that my own Lyuda had still been asleep. Fortunately, the guards had given me puzzled looks but no trouble as I slunk through the halls back to our tower.

It seemed I could do as I liked, as long as I returned safely from the excursion.

"Yes." With a yawn, I sank onto my bed. "I rode a dragon, saw Merric, and only returned just now. But no, I didn't bring him back." The admission made me wince.

"Why not?" Pippa's brows dipped into a V. "Doesn't he want to—"

"What happened?" Calli sat beside me, her gentle voice cutting off Pippa's insistent questions.

"Of course he wants to escape." I softened my tone. "But I don't know how. Their cells are built on an island, accessible only by underground tunnels."

Calli patted my knee with a sympathetic hum. "But you did see him?"

"Yes." My shoulders sagged with exhaustion. "He is alive and as well as one can be in a prison, I suppose. He was grateful for the blanket and food."

"How grateful?" Rose waggled her eyebrows, pulling her vanity stool near my bed.

Calli frowned at her. "He's in prison, Rose."

She shrugged. "Prison or not, it's still a rather romantic nighttime rendezvous."

I sighed and sat more fully on the bed so I could lean against my pillow. "He was as grateful as you would expect someone who's cold and hungry to be." His warm looks and gentle touch on my hand surely rose from feelings of gratitude, nothing of a romantic nature.

"But how did he get caught?" Pippa perched at the foot of my bed, pulling her knees to her chest.

"It seems he made it to the dragons and even spoke to them. He was so close." My fists clenched at the thought of how near we'd been to freedom. "His plan almost worked. But Leonnar managed to shout a new command at the dragons while they were still able to hear him, and they gagged Merric before he could respond."

"Those poor dragons." Calli shook her head. "Imagine how that felt, to be set free only to be captured again a moment later."

Where once I would've protested, now I nodded. Despite my reluctance, I was starting to believe Merric's explanation that the Tsantarian dragons were trapped in a far worse predicament than our own.

"So now what do we do?" Jo shuffled into our circle and flopped onto the rug.

"I need to get to the dragons." Four surprised gazes fixed on me. "Merric taught me enough phrases in *CxIyVhAuNz*—the dragon language—that I think I can set them free."

Calli hugged my arm. "Our clever Em."

"But how do we prevent Leonnar from reclaiming them again?" Rose crossed her arms over her chest.

I bit my lip. "Merric and I discussed that. We thought if I could put something in their ears to muffle sound after I've given my own instructions, hopefully they wouldn't hear anything Leonnar tried to shout at them."

"Why not just send them off after they've delivered us back to our tower?" Pippa bounced, making the mattress vibrate.

"I think their directives include returning to Yrtulk Citadel, so I don't know if they'd be free to follow my commands until they're back in Tsantar. And Merric said there are three additional dragons who aren't sent to us. In order for our plan to work, Leonnar can't have any more dragons under his control."

"And we can't save Merric from here in our tower." Calli rubbed my shoulder.

"Right." Pippa's posture drooped.

Jolene raised her head. "I have just the thing." She smiled more brightly than I'd seen in months. "I'll crochet some circles that you should be able to lodge in their ears. Then they can use their claws to remove them later."

Expectant silence filled the chamber, everyone's gazes alternating between me and Jo.

I huffed a laugh. "That sounds perfect. Thank you, Jo. One less obstacle to overcome in our plan to thwart Leonnar."

Jolene shrugged. "Of course." She hopped up and headed to her crate of yarn.

"Jo will make the ear plug things, Em needs to talk to the dragons…" Rose ticked tasks off on her fingers. "I'm assuming someone will need to free Merric on what will hopefully be our last visit to Tsantar?"

"I'll take care of that." Calli's declaration was serene but determined.

"Calli, no." I turned to her, horrified. "It's far too dangerous. How would you get onto the island? And back again?"

"You want to save him, don't you?" Her thin brows rose in perfect arches.

"Of course." Even if it meant returning to Tsantar again and again. Even if it meant our plan would fail.

"Well, you can hardly free the dragons and Merric at the same time."

"Calli would seem the least suspicious of any of us." Rose shifted on her stool. "They'd probably believe her if she said she was there to distribute baked goods or flowers to brighten the prisoners' days."

The mental image surprised a giggle from me. "But are you sure, Calli? I could find a way—"

"We owe it to him, Em." She placed a gentle hand on my arm. "And we already know you'd never be able to teach me to command the dragons. It's the best we can do."

"All right." Dread choked my throat at the thought of Calli becoming a captive in that very prison. But she radiated confidence in her plan, and she was more clever than most people gave her credit for. Perhaps her sweetness and tranquility would give the guards a false sense of trust. "Then you should make the most of the disturbance that's sure to arise when I set the dragons free."

Calli nodded, her lips pursed.

"I, meanwhile, will distract Leonnar." Rosalind tossed her hair behind her shoulder.

I leaned forward. "What do you mean? Be careful, Rose. Don't—"

She carelessly flicked a hand. "Goodness, nothing that will put me in danger. But the mere power of my full attention can be quite distracting, or so I'm told. I'll convince him I want a chance with the Crown Prince in your absence."

Calli smiled. "I'm not sure Matvey will give you up so easily."

"All the better." Rose tipped her head. "I can play them off of each other. If they're both busy trying to impress me, they'll spend less time wondering what's happening elsewhere in the citadel."

I huffed a breath. "That is a fair point. I suppose you'll have to convince them Calli and I are off on a visit to another kingdom or something to explain our absence."

Rose frowned, shaking her head. "You'll both be sick to your stomachs. Even controlling Leonnar couldn't complain about you missing a party under those circumstances. Plus, it gives me, Jo, and Pippa an excuse to make a hasty retreat if needed."

"Nausea, it is." Calli gave a dramatic wince.

"What about me?" Pippa looked uncharacteristically young and timid, curled up at the end of my bed.

I met her gaze. "You dance and have a splendid time. Act like you always do."

She straightened, her mouth puckering to a pout. "But I—"

"It's an important job, Pippa." I scrambled for an explanation. "Leonnar has commented on how well you and his brother seem to get along. If he sees you and Danil enjoying time together as usual, that will be the best way to convince him nothing strange is going on."

If all goes well, you might never see Danil again after that night. But to point that out would only make her sad or unsettled in a way that could endanger our plan.

Pippa toyed with the end of her hair, apparently considering my words.

Calli chimed in. "And Jo has been longing to teach you how to crochet. I'm sure she'd appreciate help with the ear plugs."

"Fine." Pippa slid off the bed in a languid motion and slumped toward Jolene's tangle of yarn.

"Then it's settled." Rose stood from her stool. "We make our move the next time Leonnar sends his dragons?"

Calli nodded to her, then turned to me with a reassuring smile. "We'll save Merric, and those dragons, before it's too late."

Or go up in flames trying.

Now what? FlAuVhIy had let Calli descend from her back at a quiet square in the city that stretched out from the front entrance of the citadel. She planned to approach as a commoner from the royal city, clutching a basket of food and other provisions for the prisoners.

Give her success, Maker.

The idea that two of the people I cared about most would be trapped in Leonnar's prison made me shudder, but I unclenched my jaw. I'd have to make my peace with Calli's role in this plan, because I had my own job to do.

FlAuVhIy had left me on the portion of the beach farthest from the citadel. In the distance, the island prison loomed like a dark monster rising from the waves. I longed to go to Merric to reassure him and tell him our plan. To make sure Leonnar hadn't done anything to him in the past two days.

But there was no time.

I prowled across the pebbles, feeling like a spy in my simple black attire. Tiny stones clattered as my foot slipped, bouncing until they splashed in the shallow water. I winced. Just because I looked like a spy didn't mean I had the skills necessary for the trade.

I held my breath, but no one responded to the noise. Proceeding with more caution, I picked my way across the beach toward the lights of the citadel.

GtOeBr. JpAuFlIy FlAu SmIyVh. CxAuGt. IrBrIyFlOeWd AuCx NzOeQk Tsantar. I let the words I needed to say to the dragons cycle through me, creating a rhythm for my steps. If I didn't get them just right, all of this would be for nothing. The pack at my side bulged with Jolene's ear plugs, plus a few misshapen offerings from Pippa.

Do this for them, Emelia. Give your sisters a future without Leonnar's threats and scheming.

My resolve strengthened just in time for the stables—if you could call them that—housing the dragons to come into view. I paused, taking in the enormous structure. Its scope and design would've been impressive, except it looked more like a prison than a stable. Dark stone, chains, narrow openings for light and air. And despite its size, when I pictured fitting eight dragons inside...

They must barely have room to turn around.

Something pinched in my chest. Merric felt strongly that they deserved better treatment, and he certainly had enough experience with them to know. And my own time with *FlAuVhIy* demonstrated a softer side to the imposing creatures.

We really do need to accomplish this as much for their sakes as for our own.

With a fortifying breath, I continued forward. Would I truly manage to get past the guards where Merric had failed?

But as I got a closer view, it appeared our timing had worked out as I'd hoped. As far as I could tell, the nearest stalls were empty.

I crept closer, staying to the shadows and watching the guards with narrowed eyes. They seemed relaxed enough, not glancing my way as they called to each other from their various posts.

Edging my way toward the first stall, I tucked myself into a little alcove that held rope, shovels, and a bin of what I could only assume were dead rodents based on the stink. The dragons' equivalent of a tack room, apparently. Keeping my breaths shallow, I chose a corner where I could still see out. As long as no one needed supplies, I should be safe until...

The guards' gazes shifted to the sky, and they hurried into action. I watched, muscles tense. *This is your chance, Em.* My eyes darted restlessly from the scurrying guards to the dragons landing on the flat, rocky area at the front of the stables.

One by one, the dragons were closed into their stalls. *Their cells.* At last, the guards made their way to the end of the row.

My heart trembled in my chest, pumping faster than those dragons had ever beat their wings. Three guards hauled open a thin slab of stone that acted as a door for the nearest enclosure. When they turned their attention to the final dragon, I made my move.

Springing forward but keeping my steps light, I scurried into the stall. Fumbling in the darkness, I squinted for anything to hide behind. The far corner held a nest-like pile of straw. *Good enough.*

I dove into the straw, choking against the scratchy feel and overwhelming smell, just as the dragon's huge frame shadowed the scant light coming from the opening.

The guards grumbled and commanded as the dragon entered, clearly seeking a sense of control without having any true authority.

But with Leonnar's dragon-speaking abilities, no doubt the dragon would enter its own prison without any prompting from the guards.

I shook my head. *Not after tonight.*

The guards shoved the door closed, and I took a moment to relish my success. *I did it.* I'd made it into the dragon stalls without detection.

But my job was far from over.

Sending up a prayer for Calli, hopefully in the tunnels leading to the prison, and my other sisters who must now be explaining our absence to Leonnar, I slowly lifted my head from the straw. How fitting that I'd ended up with Indigo Scales, the very dragon whose presence had haunted me for so many months.

I rose slowly, trying not to startle her. Was it a her? I couldn't quite pinpoint why, but the dragon possessed a similar sort of air as *FlAuVbIy*, making me guess she was. But although I could now admit this dragon wasn't the enemy I'd assumed, whether male or female this creature could destroy me in an instant if I wasn't careful.

Based on the sounds of chomping and slurping coming from the direction of her head, Indigo Scales was likely enjoying a snack after her riderless flight. Suppressing a shudder, I crept out of the straw. When I reached her shoulder just in front of her wing, I paused. With distance from both her swatting tail and fire-breathing mouth, this was as good a place as any to make my presence known.

Taking in a shaky breath, I placed a hand on her back. "Indigo Scales?" I had no idea if she knew my nickname for her, but hopefully she'd at least recognize my voice. "It's me, Princess Emelia."

Her head jerked toward me, but no flames. So far, so good.

I kept my voice low, hoping the other dragons' snorts and shifting hay would mask my presence from the guards. "I'm here to help."

Her expression seemed wary but less rigid than usual. Perhaps because she wasn't currently following unwanted orders.

"*GtOeBr.*" *Wait for the others.*

Her eyes widened at my use of *CxIyVhAuNz.* Hopefully that meant the words were at least recognizable, if not perfectly pronounced.

"*JpAuFlIy FlAu SmIyVh. CxAuGt. IrBr IyFlOeWd AuCx NzOeQk Tsantar.*" *Get me and my sisters home. Protect us. Then fly away and be free from Tsantar.*

She looked away, then back at my face. Caution mixed with hope seemed to simmer in those large eyes.

I reached into my bag. "And here's something to make sure Leonnar can't call you back this time."

She leaned closer as I removed two of the crocheted spheres. I pointed to her ear. "May I—?" I mimicked stuffing the lumpy circle inside.

Back to charades.

She reared her head back, apparently not yet convinced.

"So you can't hear." I covered my own ear. "But you can take it back out eventually." I curved my finger and hooked one of the loops, pulling it upward.

She nodded and lowered her head once more. Holding my breath, I inserted the plugs into one ear, then the other.

She snorted, and I tensed. Had I crossed a line? Would she—

Then she laid her chin on my shoulder. Tears pricked my eyes as I stroked the rough scales on her forehead. *Be free, Indigo Scales. Go live a life of your own choosing.*

In the strangest, most topsy-turvy way, I'd miss her.

CHAPTER 15

"AuCx NzOeQk Tsantar." Be *free from Tsantar.*

I'd dragged myself on my stomach through short gaps between the dragons' enclosures to deliver my message to each. Now the last in line, an unfamiliar dragon with dark pink scales, gave me a similar look of concern and hope that each dragon had worn as I uttered the final words Merric had taught me. Fearful of Leonnar's reaction if they were to get caught again. Fearful of control under a new Dragon Speaker. But hopefully also dreaming of freedom as a real possibility.

Almost time for the next step.

With another set of bumbling gestures and calming words that no doubt sounded like nonsense, Fuchsia Scales allowed me to insert the last of the plugs into her ears. *Please, let them be enough.*

With a firm nod, I gestured to the rock slab at the front of the stall. She seemed to catch my meaning, tensing her muscles with an expression of grim determination.

Panic gripped my stomach in tight claws. What if the dragons weren't strong enough to—?

Fuchsia Scales rammed into the slab, swinging it open like a hinged door. Apparently, there was no cause for concern on that front.

As though waiting for that sign, more crashes sounded down the row as dragons forced open their heavy makeshift doors. Outside, guards started running and shouting.

Call for reinforcements from the prison. Please. I sent up a quick prayer for Calli and Merric but couldn't pause to consider their predicament.

I was in a predicament of my own.

I jogged out of the stall, trying to hide in the shadows. But despite the surrounding chaos, a guard spotted me.

"Stop! Stop her!" Several other guards heard the call, their gazes flying between me and the escaping dragons.

Before I could flee, hands clamped on my arms. I writhed against the grip, only to have a second guard put a sword to my throat.

I froze, struggling to swallow. *Watch for an opportunity, Em.* And if none came... It was worth it if my sisters, Merric, and these dragons all gained their freedom.

Guards slung ropes at the dragons, attempted to pierce them with swords and arrows. But their scales were just as impenetrable as Leonnar boasted. More guards appeared every moment, drawn by the shouts and commotion. I watched the nearest door, knowing who must be running down the corridors at this very moment.

Seconds later, Leonnar erupted from the citadel, his face dark with fury. He shouted a string of words in *CxIyVhAuNz* I didn't bother to translate. I watched the dragons, waiting for a reaction. Could they hear him? Their movements didn't change as they flew higher, circling the stables much as they'd circled our tower at Kavalya Palace.

Leonnar's face grew increasingly red as he shouted himself hoarse, striding closer to the dragons. The ear plugs were working. The guard who held my arms adjusted his grip as I sagged in relief.

Emerald Scales and Peach Scales shifted course, but they didn't even glance at their screaming former master. Instead, they headed toward the citadel. Scarlet and Golden followed suit. To the balcony? I had instructed them to bring my sisters back to Oneska. But where did my sisters plan to go? Why hadn't we discussed this? I bit my lip, wanting to close my eyes but unable to tear my gaze away.

On the ground, guards shot larger projectiles at the remaining dragons. One hit Fuchsia Scales, seeming to produce more anger than injury. An exhale of flame lit a nearby tree on fire, and more shouts rose calling for water.

Why, Leonnar? Why couldn't you be content to rule your own kingdom well without snatching at power in other countries? Why did you have to use dragons for your own ends instead of letting them live in peace?

As if drawn by my thoughts, Leonnar's seething gaze collided with mine. My hands trembled, but I refused to flinch. If he wanted to continue this vendetta against Oneska, let it be out in the open without secret dealings. Without dragons to fight his battles for him.

Oneska—and their Crown Princess—would no longer cower in fear.

Leonnar stalked toward me, but movement in the sky drew my eyes upward. Rose, Jo, and Pippa rode their dragons high above. *Thank you, Maker.* Wherever they'd ended up, the dragons had found them. Now if only Calli...

"What have you done?" If Leonnar could spout flames, I'd be a raging inferno. "Do you know what you've just unleashed on the world? The destructive, vile deeds they'll do now that—"

"The destructive, vile deeds have all been yours, Prince Leonnar. I understand now that the dragons were only following your commands. But no longer." My smile was more genuine than I would've imagined I could produce when captured by an enemy kingdom.

He growled. "I may have lost them, but I have you. Imagine what your father might be willing to do to free you from our prison."

Following his tense lead, my guards tugged me away from the stables. Ahead, an iron door led into a portion of the citadel that looked more jagged, less polished than the balcony and ballroom. The tunnels to the prison? It hung ajar, faint torchlight illuminating the passage within. I glanced around, willing my eyes to pierce the surrounding darkness.

Had Calli and Merric—?

Two figures emerged from the door, talking and laughing as though taking a casual stroll. The taller silhouette limped a bit on the uneven terrain. Merric? Was he hurt or just weak from so many days in prison? I wanted to scream at them to run, but drawing Leonnar's notice would only put them in more danger.

Hoping to create a diversion, I tripped. "Ouch." I let my ankle buckle beneath me, dragging me down. The sword tip still pointed at my neck pricked harder. The guards hauled me to my feet.

Leonnar scowled. "Get up, you clumsy girl. I don't have time for your—"

"Unhand her!" Merric changed his trajectory. My heart both lifted and convulsed at the concern in his voice.

Much as I wanted him to save me, I'd rather he save himself.

"Em." Calli hurried behind him.

No, no, no. Don't drag yourselves into this. You were so close. I shook my head. "Run! Get away from here, please." The last word came out as a sob.

Leonnar glanced my way, then studied my intended rescuers more closely. "Princess Callista? Also not ill, I see." Disdain dripped from his tone. "Seize them."

The guard with the sword left my side, heading for Calli.

Leonnar gripped Merric's arm. "I hope you enjoyed your brief reprieve from our prison. It will be your last."

Merric stomped on his foot, wrenching free from his grip. "Emelia—"

Flapping wings drew our attention to the sky once more. *FlAuVhIy* hovered above us, ire in her gaze.

Leonnar's expression lit. *No. FlAuVhIy* didn't have earplugs and likely didn't realize he was a Dragon Speaker. My panicked mind landed on the words I needed as he opened his mouth to give a command. I gestured frantically to Merric and Calli.

"*JpAuFlIy IyNz SmIyVh. CxAuGt IyNz.*" *Get Merric and my sister home. Protect them.*

With a surprised look at me, she nodded her enormous head. Swatting away the guard who'd laid hold of Calli, she swept Merric and Calli onto her back.

Leonnar recovered from his shock with a grunt. "*SmOe—*" Before he could complete the word, I lurched forward and knocked him off balance.

Merric said something to *FlAuVhIy*, and she ascended out of hearing range.

"Emelia, no!" Calli's cry drifted into the night as they left my view, their anxious gazes latched onto me.

They're safe. I almost laughed, despite the guard who was once again bruising my arms with his grip. Prince Leonnar had lost any semblance of his polished veneer.

He turned to me, eyes wild with rage. "You will pay dearly for this, Princess Emelia." The title sounded more mocking than a formality. "Your entire kingdom will pay…"

A blast of flame lit the night, setting Leonnar's cloak ablaze. He shrieked, and the guards released me to help their prince.

I looked up, dizzy with confusion, fear, and exhaustion. *Indigo Scales.*

She hovered close enough to allow me to latch onto her scales and drag myself up onto her back. Gripping her scales tightly, I crawled to her neck while she gained altitude.

Below, guards continued to shout while Leonnar screamed profanities.

I collapsed against Indigo's neck. "You came back for me." Tears choked my voice, even though I knew she couldn't hear me.

My sisters were each accounted for. Merric was out of prison. Indigo had literally snatched me from Leonnar's clutches.

As clumsy as our efforts may have been, we were free.

My limbs trembled as I clung to my dragon. "Thank you."

I squeezed Calli in another hug. "I can still hardly believe we're all here. And safe. With the threat of dragons gone."

I'd bid goodbye to Indigo Scales at our tower, then cried even harder when I returned to our chamber to see my sisters all safe and well. According to Calli, Merric had been ready to command *FlAuVhIy* to bring him back to Tsantar until he saw me return atop my dragon. He'd bid us a timid goodnight, looking ready to collapse into his own bed.

Despite our exhaustion, I doubted my sisters and I would get any sleep tonight.

"We are so blessed." Calli squeezed me tight, her smile glowing.

I kept an arm about her shoulders where we sat together on her bed. "But how did you manage to free Merric? I was so worried…"

"About me?" A giggle shook her back. "I had the easiest job of us all."

Rosalind snorted from where she lounged on the floor. "Sneaking prisoners out of dungeons. It doesn't get much easier than that."

Pippa snickered, leaning forward with wide eyes.

"The guards weren't so bad. Those poor prisoners, though…" Calli's voice softened to a whisper. "I was tempted to free more than just Merric."

"Go back to the beginning." Rose seemed either unaware of or unconcerned with Calli's sudden emotion. "How did you manage it?"

Calli shrugged. "I showed them my basket and said it was for the prisoners. They offered to deliver the food for me, but of course I refused. I told them the prisoners needed my prayers even more than the supplies."

"You offered to pray with them?" Such a thing would've never occurred to me. Calli really had been the right one for the task all along.

"Certainly. Who could need prayer more than convicted criminals? Besides—"

"And they let you in, just like that?" Rose's incredulous tone cut her off.

"No, they had questions for me. And they insisted on sifting through the basket." Calli tipped her head back, as though studying the stars through our ceiling. "We talked for some time. The guards really were quite pleasant once I got past their gruff exteriors."

"Only you could manage that in the first place." Rose shook her head.

"What a nice idea, Calli. Even though you were trying to free Merric, I'm sure the prisoners appreciated your supplies and prayers." Jo's soft voice rose from her pile of cushions on the floor.

"But how did you get to Merric?" Hopefully I didn't sound *too* preoccupied with his role in her story.

"Well, eventually they did let me pray with the prisoners. I prayed with every one." Pride rang out in her voice. *Sweet Calli.* "A few weren't very welcoming, but several of them were quite grateful. I prayed extra hard when I came to Merric, and I tried to include a few hints about what was happening elsewhere in the citadel. The guards weren't paying very close attention by then."

She turned to me. "Your commotion with the dragons made the rest simple. I'd spotted the ring of keys for each cell while I talked with the guards. I ran back to grab them while the guards investigated the dragons, then went straight to Merric's cell to set him free."

"You are truly a marvel, Callista." Rose's tone held both admiration and amusement.

I tightened my grip on her shoulder. "I'm just glad you're safe."

"And that my undertaking was successful." She raised her brows, a new light glittering in her eyes.

My stomach sank with the weight of a hundred pebbles. Thank heavens our mission was a success, and we were all home and safe. But how much bonding had occurred between Calli and Merric as she rescued him?

Calli's forehead furrowed as she studied me more closely. *Time to change the subject.*

"Did your—distraction—go as planned, Rosalind?"

"Mostly." She shifted to prop herself up with her elbows. "I'm not sure whether Leonnar fell for any of it, but in the end it didn't matter. The man is so conceited that he couldn't resist the draw of a lady's compliments, even while he suspected I was up to something." She fluffed her hair. "Especially a lady who is so very fair and sought after."

"Matvey was less than pleased." Pippa puckered her lips to one side.

"True." Rose shrugged. "But as I hoped, Leonnar only seemed more interested in holding my attention once he saw how much it bothered his brother."

"They never stood a chance." I suppressed a grin, catching Calli's amused gaze.

Calli winked before turning back to Rose. "We're so grateful you were able to keep Leonnar occupied without putting yourself in peril. And Jo, your crocheted ear plugs must've worked!" She turned to me. "At least I'm assuming they did, since the dragons got away."

My breath released in a relieved puff. "Yes, they were very effective. The size and shape were perfect. Hopefully now the dragons won't have too much trouble getting them out again."

"I wonder what the dragons will do, now that they're no longer under Leonnar's control." Calli's sad tone reflected my own disappointment at saying goodbye to the dragons so soon after they'd become our allies.

"Enjoy peace, adventure, family." Rose stretched her arm across Jolene's back. "And freedom. Just like we'll get to do."

CHAPTER 16

"THERE YOU ARE. YOUR sisters said I might find you here."

"Merric." My hands fumbled, nearly dropping the embroidery I held in my lap. The events of the night before felt more like a vivid nightmare than reality, but here was Merric, back at the palace. *Safe.*

But what was I supposed to say to him now that our ordeal was over? Especially since... My heart raced at the memory of our late breakfast with Father. Led by Calli, my sisters had given a stumbling account of a brave stable hand sending away the dragons with a mysterious language.

Did Merric know yet? Did he—?

"It's so good to see you well, after..." He lowered his head in concern. "But *are* you well?"

"Of course." My smile was genuine, if hesitant. "I never have to go to Tsantar again. Never have to dance with Prince Leonnar again."

"I think I'm almost as happy about that fact as you are."

My nervous giggle sounded more like it emanated from Pippa. "I apologize if you couldn't find me. Sometimes I prefer to work outside in nice weather. The sunlight provides good illumination, and my sisters are lovely but on occasion I appreciate a break..."

I needed to stop talking before the poor man went running in the opposite direction.

"I can understand that. I prefer the outdoors as well." Merric adjusted his hat, then frowned. "Should I remove my hat in the company of royalty? I'm never sure..."

"It doesn't bother me."

"Ah. Good." He shifted, his fists clenching and unclenching. "Do you mind if I join you?"

"Not at all." I unnecessarily slid farther over on the bench I occupied in the garden.

"Thank you." He sat but seemed poised to escape at a moment's notice.

I risked a glance at him. "Was there a reason you were looking for me?"

His chuckle was endearing in its awkwardness. "Actually, yes." He ran his palms over his riding breeches. "I just left an audience with your father."

"Oh?" My gaze fastened to my embroidery, as though my very life depended on the precision of each stitch. *Coward.*

"Yes, I was quite surprised by the summons. It seems your sisters shared the news about the disappearance of the dragons, giving me far too much credit in the process."

"Not too much credit, surely." I finally managed to meet his eye. "We never could've done it without you."

"Well, I could at least understand why they minimized the role each of you played in the feat. Your father was so thrilled, fortunately he accepted their explanation without many questions." He gripped the edge of the wooden bench, his cheeks reddening. "But now he seems to think I've earned his reward."

"I see." My heart quivered like the wings of a bug stuck in water. "Do you plan to accept?"

"I'm considering it." He cleared his throat. "It isn't every day a stable hand like me is offered a princess's hand in marriage, after all. I'd hate to offend the king by turning it down."

My hands trembled in my lap. *Look him in the eye, Emelia. You at least owe him that much.* Jaw tense, I raised my head. "I wish you and Callista every happiness. Truly. She will—"

"Callista?" His frown was part amusement, part bewilderment. "What makes you think I'd choose to marry her?"

"She saved you from the prison! She's so sweet, and the two of you get along so well. I just assumed..." I rattled my brain for a coherent thought to complete the statement, but none were to be found.

He tilted his head, donning a ghost of a grin that made me both want to kiss him and shove him. "She is very sweet. So much so that I could never do her the great injustice of requesting her hand in marriage when she'd much prefer that duke of hers."

I attempted to turn my unladylike snort into a cough. "Duke Virkalt? They do enjoy spending time together, but how could she prefer him when you're around?" The implication of my words hit me a moment too late, and I resumed my stitching with vehemence, face ablaze.

"She does seem to prefer him quite a lot, and I'm glad of it. But I appreciate your high valuation of my merit as a potential suitor." He edged a bit closer, making it hard to swallow.

"As a suitor for Calli, yes." By this point, I'd missed so many stitches I'd have to scrap the project entirely if this painful conversation ever came to an end. "Then you must have Rosalind in mind. For yourself, that is." Why couldn't I put together just one intelligent sentence in this man's presence?

"Rosalind, hmm?" Every fiber of my being was on high alert as he reached behind me to pluck a glowing coral dahlia blossom from its stem. "An interesting suggestion, but I confess she's never crossed my mind."

I grimaced when my needle struck my forefinger, drawing blood. "She's generally considered the prettiest of the family."

"Is she, indeed? I hadn't noticed." He tucked the flower behind my ear, then took my hand and gently wrapped a handkerchief around my injury. His thumb stroked my wrist as he leaned close. "I'd hate for this to taint your lovely embroidery."

I set the hoops aside before he could see the mess I'd made of what was supposed to become a sprig of wildflowers. Or was he teasing me?

I glanced at his face. His proximity and earnest gaze made my heart rattle in my chest like a snared dragon, but I couldn't seem to look away.

He took the opportunity to snatch up my other hand. "Pleasant as your sisters are, I'll admit I've hardly noticed their charms. I've only seen *you* ever since my first encounter with your family."

"You want to marry *me*?" The very idea seemed too precious, too impossible to be spoken aloud. I pulled away, trying to shatter the dream before it could take root. "Your goal is to become king, then."

"King?" His laugh held a note of bitterness. "Is that what you think of me? I'd far prefer to keep my position as a stable hand, if it were merely a matter of employment."

The truth of his reprimand stung. I didn't see him as the kind of man who would grasp at a throne, and the accusation was unfair. "No, I'm sorry. But why, then?" I cringed at the frailty of my quiet voice, the bluntness of the question. But if I was going to marry Merric, share my life with him, I had to know. "I've only ever forced you to work with me and Lyuda under false pretenses, accused you, scolded you, lashed out in anger and fear, gotten you imprisoned... You couldn't possibly care for me." I stood, hoping desperately my legs would support me. "And I'd rather not—"

"Is that the trouble?" He rose too, his voice amused but gentle. "You care fiercely for your family, Emelia. For your kingdom. You were right to take your time in trusting me, especially when the other man in your life who could communicate with dragons was such a tyrant." Venom seeped from the word. "I was concerned that day on the trail when I heard you speaking *CxIyVhAuNz*. But also impressed beyond all imagining. There's a reason humans only learn the dragon language with the help of magic. The fact you made so much progress without it was awe-inspiring. If not a little terrifying."

I turned toward where he now stood at a respectful distance. "So you're choosing me because I intimidate you."

He narrowed his eyes. "I'm choosing you because I'm fascinated by you. Mesmerized by you. Callista may be sweet, Rosalind may be beautiful, but you, Emelia, have a spark that draws me like a luna moth to a candle. Without my immensely good fortune in earning your father's reward, I would've kept wandering kingdom after kingdom, unable to find another woman to compare with you."

I closed my eyes against the doubts assailing me. Leonnar had only used and threatened me. No other man had ever shown the least interest in *me*, rather than my position as the eldest princess. Was it possible Merric could want me? In spite of my rank rather than because of it? The burn of tears made me flinch. I couldn't cry before...

The thought dissipated like mist on a breeze. Why couldn't I cry before Merric? He thought I was strong, smart, interesting. He wanted to marry me. *But...* I sniffled and backed away.

He didn't let me get far. A fresh handkerchief appeared in his hand. *How many does the man carry?* "Em. You've been strong for your family for so long. But you're safe now. Your sisters are safe. Let yourself lean on someone else for once. I'd be honored to take on that task for the rest of our lives." He studied my gaze as he dabbed at the tears on my cheeks. "Would you consider marrying me, Emelia? I've fallen quite desperately in love with you. But no matter what your father says, I'd never force you—"

"Yes." I pressed my forehead against his shoulder. *Yes, please.*

With an erratic breath, he circled his arms around my back. He smelled like soap and dragon fire and pine needles and home.

I tipped my head back just enough to look into his face. "You won't make me ride dragons, will you?"

His laugh blew across my cheeks. "Only when I want to whisk you away from the palace."

A shiver whispered over my shoulders at the intensity that darkened his golden gaze for a moment before he grinned. "But the more important question is, can that poor embroidery be salvaged, do you think? Even I could see those last few stitches were quite dreadful."

I blinked, then pinched his arm as his meaning sank in. "Let me go, you exasperating Dragon Speaker."

His grip tightened on my back. "Soon, my beautiful dancer. I was very much hoping to kiss you first." Hope and vulnerability warred with the mischief in his eyes as they locked with mine. "If you wouldn't object."

Something leaped into my throat—my heart, perhaps—making it difficult to breathe. "Only if you take back your insult to my embroidery."

His smile came slow as he leaned close enough to make our breaths mingle. "It's the finest handiwork I've ever seen."

"Hmm, I suppose that—"

He slipped his fingers into my hair, his lips claiming mine.

Pippa dropped the pieces of her marble game as I closed the door to our chamber behind me. "Did you see Merric? He was looking for you."

The soft squeak of Jo's crochet hooks fell silent, and Rose snapped her book shut.

"Merric?" The syllables felt new and foreign on my tongue, as though I'd never spoken his name before. *My fiancé.* "I...that is, he—" I sank onto the settee across from the fireplace beside Calli, studying the rug beneath our feet as though I'd been asked to make a copy. "Yes, he found me. But don't let me disturb you all." I made a shooing motion toward the four sets of eyes that held far too much speculation.

"And?" Calli's brows rose, her face alight with anticipation. "Did he say anything about Father's reward?"

My heart wrung like a dishrag in my chest. Was I about to disappoint her?

Rosalind abandoned her perch on her bed and approached, bending to study me. "I'd imagine yes based on your blush. Come on, out with it, then." She settled on the floor at my feet like a child eager for a story.

Hopefully I wouldn't be disappointing any of her expectations, either.

Breathe, Emelia. Just say it. "He did bring up the reward."

"I knew it." Rose rested her chin on her folded hands.

Jo and Pippa both edged closer, choosing spots near Rose on the rug.

I darted a guilty glance at Calli, who appeared as serene as usual. Why couldn't I hide my emotions like that? "It seems he wants to marry...me." I grasped her hands. "I'm so sorry if that dashes your hopes. I'm as shocked as anyone, but—"

"Shocked?" Calli's musical laugh seemed genuine. "I doubt anyone else is. Why should I be disappointed?"

It couldn't possibly be this simple. "But the two of you got along so well. You were always so much kinder to him, and you saved him from the prison. It would only be natural if you'd come to care for each other."

Calli patted my knee in a gesture that suddenly made me feel like the younger sister. "I care for Merric very much as a friend and future brother. It's never been anything more than that. Merric is perfect for you. He'll make you very happy, if you let him." A hint of mirth cut through her sincerity as she held my gaze.

Rose flung a pillow at me. "Calli's got Duke Virkalt ready to propose any day, she never needed Merric. Anyone with eyes could see he's been smitten with you all along. What a relief you finally know about it and return the poor man's feelings." She straightened, her forehead wrinkling in alarm. "You did say yes, didn't you?"

"I did." I buried my face in the convenient pillow as my sisters squealed. If I'd been blushing before, now the heat in my skin blazed like a furnace.

"Oh, you two will be so adorable and yet so painful to be around now that you're fully declared lovebirds." Rose heaved a dramatic sigh.

I peeked out from my sanctuary. "You don't mind, do you, Rosie? I know you find him handsome—"

"Bah." She waved away my concern with a regal swat. "Thank goodness he's handsome, for I couldn't bear to have an ugly man hanging about us all the time. And I'm only sixteen, after all. I plan to be surrounded by many handsome men before I make my choice someday."

Calli and I shared a glance that was half-amused, half-exasperated. A weight lifted from my shoulders at the familiar exchange. If she didn't hold any resentment toward me for being Merric's choice, then my joy truly would be complete.

Rosalind leaned forward. "Jo and Pippa didn't want to marry him either, so you can stop stalling and tell us already—did he kiss you?"

"Rose! That's hardly appropriate to discuss..." I tilted my head toward our younger sisters, who were latched onto every word of our conversation.

"I knew it." Rose settled back with a smile like a satisfied cat. "The pins in your hair look a bit looser than before." She picked a stray thread off her skirt. "Merric's going to be smiling for months, as long as you don't turn cold and harsh toward him again."

The heat flared yet again as my memory sank back into Merric's warm embrace. Blinking, I shook my head. "That's quite enough..."

"It's all right, Em." Pippa rose to a crouch to tap my knee. "You'll probably be kissing Merric a lot if you're going to marry him. You might as well enjoy it."

Jolene's peal of laughter echoed the loudest as my sisters showered me with hugs and congratulations.

"I'm sorry this has taken you away from your role as a stable hand." Merric and I had left Kirill and Lyuda behind in the clearing and now picked our way up the ragged path leading to *FlAuVbIy*'s cave.

A full week had passed since the announcement of our engagement, and the time had been filled with fittings, wedding preparations, parties, and other social events, leaving us hardly a moment to ourselves. Today, we'd taken an opportunity to sneak off on our own.

Merric paused, brows drawn. "What makes you think that bothers me?"

I made my way over an exposed tree root. "I know you miss the horses."

He shrugged. "Fortunately, my fiancée is a fine horsewoman, so I hope there will be many rides in our future."

"True." At a wider section of path, I turned to face him. "But you've also tugged at your collar at least five times since you tied up Kirill."

"Ah." He once again pulled the offending collar away from his neck. "The transition from stable hand to future prince will take a bit more getting used to, I'll admit. And the next time that tailor insists on making me more 'royalty-appropriate' clothing, I'll talk with him about these collars. But they can't stop me from wearing my favorite hat, at least when I'm outside." He tilted his hat to a jaunty angle, then grasped my hand and drew me closer. "And I get to spend the rest of my life with you, Emelia. I wouldn't trade that for the world."

I twined my fingers with his. "I just hope you won't end up regretting it someday."

"Not possible." He released my hand to circle an arm around my waist, his other thumb tracing a gentle line from my temple to my jaw. "A life by your side is where I want to be. Even if it means I have to be a prince."

He cut my giggle short with a kiss. I clutched the fine material of his new jacket, pulling him closer.

After a few breathless moments, I stepped back. "Did you actually plan to visit *FlAuVbIy* today, or were you just trying to get us some privacy?"

He closed the gap between us. "Both." His whisper at my ear sent a pleasant thrill down my back.

"Not that I'm complaining." I tipped my head back, and he took the invitation for a deeper kiss, holding me close. I savored his warmth, his love, this opportunity to focus on *us*.

To focus on joy rather than the fear and worry of protecting my sisters and kingdom from Tsantar.

With a sigh, he released me, pressing one final kiss to my forehead. "I suppose we should continue to *FlAuVbIy*." His voice came out a bit hoarse.

"We have come all this way, after all." I twined my arm with his, leaning against his side.

We reached *FlAuVbIy*'s cave in companionable silence, taking in the beauty of the crisp autumn day.

Merric called a greeting, and she hurried out of the cave. If dragons could smile, she was beaming.

I let her and Merric converse without interruption, not bothering to pick out any familiar words. A hawk soared overhead, making lazy circles beneath the puffy white clouds.

Merric took my hand. "Do you want to say hi?"

"Of course." I followed him closer to the large ebony dragon.

"Hi *FlAuVbIy*. It's good to see you well." I patted the gleaming scales on her neck.

Merric translated, then *FlAuVbIy* spoke again. "She is glad to see you, too. And to see us together." His cheeks reddened as he gave me a shy grin.

"A matchmaking dragon, eh? She'll get along with my sisters."

Merric chuckled as he said something else to *FlAuVbIy*, then turned back to me. "Shall we?"

My pulse jogged a bit faster, but only with anticipation. No fear. "Yes."

Merric helped me up onto her back. With a final instruction to the dragon—knowing Merric, it was a request, not a command—he clambered up after me. His arms looped around my waist, and I settled back against his chest.

Yes, I think flying will be much more pleasant from now on.

I tensed, turning my head toward Merric. "We'd better not go anywhere near Kavalya Palace. My poor father..."

He hugged me tighter. "That's exactly what I was just telling her."

Exhaling my relief, I relaxed against him. "Thank you."

"He's safe now. You're all safe. I wouldn't do anything to jeopardize your kingdom's newfound security."

I rubbed my thumb across his hand, a rush of gratitude cutting off my voice. Ever since this man had unwittingly stumbled across my path, I'd gone from hopelessness to safety. From feeling the weight of full responsibility for my family and kingdom to having an equal, supportive partner.

FlAuVhIy flapped her wings, lifting from the ground. I smiled into the wind blowing tendrils of hair about my face. The orange autumn sun shone on us like a blessing from the Maker.

As we surged forward, the vibrancy of true freedom sang through my veins. Freedom from Tsantar's control, from a life of secrets and darkness and fear. Freedom to love this man with my whole heart and work together to rule Oneska with justice and compassion.

I fully intended to make the most of it.

REVIEWS

Thanks so much for taking the time to read *The Dancer and the Dragon Speaker*! If you enjoyed this adventure, please consider leaving a review on Amazon or sharing about it on social media.

Even a sentence or two will help more readers discover Princess Emelia's story. Thank you!!

THE INTERTWINED TALES

- *The Shifter and the Mage* (retelling King Thrushbeard & Little Wildrose) by Lucy Winton

- *The Caring and the Cursed* (retelling Puss in Boots & Snow White and Rose Red) by Amanda Thompson

- *The Princess and the Shoemaker* (retelling The Elves and the Shoemaker & The Red Shoes) by S.R. Nulton

- *The Fairest and the Coffin* (retelling Snow White & The Crystal Coffin) by Kendra E. Ardnek

- *The Golden Touch and the Silver Note* (retelling King Midas & The Nightingale) by Ashley Mendoza

- *The Secret and the Shadow Bride* (retelling The Goose Girl & The Shadow) by Jodie Seibert

- *The Baker and the Abandoned Mansion* (retelling Little Red Riding Hood & The Lover's Ghost) by Kathryn Radaker

- *The Dancer and the Dragon Speaker* (retelling The Twelve Dancing Princesses & The Language of the Birds) by Laurie Lucking

- *The Mermaid and the Cursed Prince* (retelling The Little Mermaid & The Crystal Ball) by E.J. Kitchens

- *The Golden Secret and the Enchanted Beast* (retelling Rumpelstiltskin & Beauty and the Beast) by C.K. Johnson

- *The Lord of Shadow and the Queen of Flames* (retelling Sleeping Beauty & The Lute Player) by Cortney Manning

- *The Mouse and the Fairy* (retelling Thumbelina & The Forest Bride) by H. Eleanor Long

NEXT IN THE INTERTWINED TALES...

A mermaid without fins. A human prince without legs. Only one curse can be broken.

When Crestfall's ambassador to the curse-prone human kingdom Birney retires, Keola is the unlucky mermaid chosen to replace him. Her bad luck changes to disaster when she's injured carrying an urgent message to her king. Her rescuer—a talking whale claiming to be a cursed prince—takes her to a feared enchantress to save her from her supposed curse of being half-fish.

Stuck with a doltish prince who might just be more than he seems, an urgent message, and no fins, Keola must join a hunt for a crystal ball to save not just her scales but both human and underwater kingdoms. Can she find it before her heart gets hopelessly tangled up with a prince who doesn't belong to the sea she loves?

The Mermaid and the Cursed Prince is a retelling of "The Little Mermaid" and "The Crystal Ball."

Available on December 13th, 2024 – preorder now!
https://www.amazon.com/gp/product/B0D77F34YX

ACKNOWLEDGEMENTS

I knew as soon as I saw Lucy Winton's idea for The Intertwined Tales that I wanted to join in, and I'm so glad I did! Lucy shepherded us through this project with so much patience and grace, and I've loved the opportunity to brainstorm and collaborate with every author in the series. I hope our writing journeys cross paths again soon!

To my readers – your enthusiasm for my earlier releases this year and anticipation leading up to *The Dancer and the Dragon Speaker* mean more to me than I can express. It's such a joy to bring a story from my mind and heart to life on the page and then share it with all of you! Thanks for entrusting me with your time and imagination.

So many thanks to my family! Taking on so many writing deadlines often meant our floors looked like a minefield littered with toys and our dirty dishes piled by the sink could've qualified as a mountain. I'm so grateful for your love, encouragement, and patience as I pursue this writing dream.

The Dancer and the Dragon Speaker would've never made it to publication-ready status in time without my fabulous beta readers, Natasha and Ms. Z-K, and my proofreader extraordinaire, Elise! Thanks for sharing everything you loved about the story in the midst of fixing my inconsistencies and errors.

All glory to God, who gave me the time and inspiration at all the right moments to pull this story together. What a gift to be living out my own fairy tale as the daughter of the Most High King!

ALSO BY LAURIE LUCKING

Tales of the Mystics

Common

Traitor (coming in 2025)

The Cornerstone Series

A Noble Purpose

Read on for the first scene!

A Noble Purpose

Sneak Peek

CHAPTER 1

"Joyous twelvemonth, dear Verena. Joyous twelvemonth to you!"

I added an exaggerated vibrato on the last note as an extra tribute to my older sister on the anniversary of her birth, but of course she didn't smile. As far as I'd seen, her lips had barely twitched upward in years.

Verena nodded her acknowledgment. "Thank you." Her gaze drooped back to the generous slice of raspberry strudel on her glossy porcelain plate.

My lady's maid, Nadette, fluttered to my side and filled my teacup with steaming amber liquid. Biting her lip, she surreptitiously tucked a stray lock of dark hair into my chignon before backing her petite frame away from the table.

"I'm so glad your favorite dessert happens to be the same as mine." I raised a forkful of strudel toward Verena, as though in a toast.

"It is delicious." She nodded, her expression more suited to a funeral than a celebration in her honor.

Pappa gave Mamma a meaningful look, and I paused mid-bite. He'd been watching Verena in growing agitation for weeks, not that she seemed to notice. But from the intensity of his pacing every time he'd studied her with that determined set of his jaw, he had to be planning something.

Something Verena would absolutely hate, if I had to guess.

Mamma's eyes narrowed as she gave her head a tiny shake, but Pappa stared her down with furrowed brows. Eventually she sighed, giving her dainty lace-bordered napkin an irritated snap as she returned it to the table.

A glance at Verena confirmed she'd missed the entire exchange, distracted with slicing her pastry into precise squares before taking polite bites.

I was already scraping the last smear of raspberry jam from my plate's scalloped edge.

"Verena." Pappa's commanding tone didn't bode well. He let his fork drop with a clatter.

She flinched and looked up. "Yes?"

"This has gone on long enough." He gestured across the table at her.

"Luncheon?" She widened her deep brown eyes—the same shade as mine and Mamma's—in a melancholy query.

I dabbed my mouth to cover a giggle. *Oh, Verena.* For all her intelligence and training, she often failed to note the mood shifts taking place around her.

Pappa gave a blustery cough. "Luncheon? No, I mean this entire attitude of yours. You are the Crown Princess of Walthar, for heaven's sake, yet you mope around like a deprived child. You have every advantage, every luxury, and you can't even be bothered to smile."

All traces of humor fled as Verena's expression changed from bland indifference to sadness. *Don't be too hard on her, Pappa.*

"It's not that I'm ungrateful, Pappa. Truly. I apologize if my behavior shames you. I try to fulfill my duties as Crown Princess, even if I can't force a cheerful demeanor." An unusual hardness edged Verena's tone.

"Except you don't." Pappa rose from his chair, replacing it with a clatter. *Time for more pacing.* "You're turning 25 years old today, Verena. Yet you've hardly spoken a word to any of the local noblemen or visiting royalty. Have you no plans to marry and produce an heir?"

If possible, Verena's shoulders sagged further.

I squeezed her hand under the table, and she clutched my fingers like a lifeline. "That's not true, Pappa. Verena was downright chatty with the Earl of Arvid last month."

Mamma directed a gentle smile my way. "The Earl of Arvid is married, Liesel."

"What?" I flicked my free hand in a dramatic wave. "How very inconvenient. Perhaps he has a brother? Or cousin?"

"There's no need for matchmaking." Verena acknowledged my feeble attempt before turning back to Pappa. "I have little interest in romance, Pappa. Surely, I can rule just fine on my own."

"With my help, of course." I bounced in my seat. "And in my first step toward becoming a royal advisor, I really must insist you finish your strudel, Pappa. I believe it is the finest Cook has made yet."

Mamma nodded, flashing me a conspiratorial wink. "She'll likely be offended if you send it back to the kitchens uneaten. Perhaps this conversation can wait for another time."

The tightness in Pappa's jaw eased, and he rejoined us at the table. "We'd never want to offend dear Cook. But I'm afraid this conversation can't wait." His gaze hardened as he turned back to Verena. "What is this about ruling alone? What about heirs to the royal line? A family? It seems matchmaking will become necessary, Verena, if you fail to find a future king on your own."

"If you wish, Pappa." Verena glanced to the tall window as her throat convulsed in a hard swallow. "But if this is about smiling more, I will try harder to appear more grateful for—"

"No." Pappa's fist collided with the polished arm of his chair. "No, that's not enough."

Mamma squeezed his shoulder. "I think what your father is tryin' to say is that we wish for you to find true happiness, not just the appearance of it."

"Precisely." He patted Mamma's hand. "But I'm at a loss as to how to accomplish that, aside from finding a man who can bring you joy where the rest of us have failed."

I leaned forward. "But if Verena doesn't want a husband, maybe a puppy could cheer her up instead. Or..."

Pappa silenced me with a look, his expression both fond and exasperated.

Mamma covered her mouth with her napkin, her cough sounding suspiciously like a giggle.

"I am quite determined. Something must be done, and I hope in time you'll thank us." Pappa stood again, regal in a silver-edged vest that matched his closely-cropped hair. "At tonight's celebration ball, we'll make a special announcement. A challenge, you might say." He raised a fist, as though practicing for the evening's event. "The first man who can make you laugh—truly laugh with real pleasure—shall earn your hand in marriage."

Want to find out what happens next? *A Noble Purpose* is a non-magical Christian fantasy retelling of Hans, Who Made the Princess Laugh. Available in ebook (including Kindle Unlimited), paperback, and hardcover!

https://www.amazon.com/Noble-Purpose-Cornerstone-Princess-Retelling-ebook/dp/B0CPZSVJ6Z

ABOUT THE AUTHOR

LAURIE LUCKING LOVES BOOKS, music, and spending time with her family in beautiful Minnesota. A recovering attorney, she now spends her days chasing her active 2-year-old, answering hundreds of questions for her kindergartener, and shuttling her sons to after-school clubs, Boy Scouts, and basketball practice (plus a little cooking and cleaning when absolutely necessary). When she finds a spare moment, she writes young adult romantic fantasy inspired by fairy tales.

Laurie's novels have won the Excellence in Editing Award and finaled in the Carol Awards. Her short stories have been published in Deep Magic e-zine, Brio magazine, and a number of anthologies. She enjoys connecting with readers through her website, www.laurieluc king.com (sign up for her newsletter to receive a free short story!), and in the Facebook group she co-founded, Faith and Fairy Tales.

www.ingramcontent.com/pod-product-compliance
Lightning Source LLC
Chambersburg PA
CBHW030143010826
48973CB00002B/705